LOOSE ENDS

LOOSE ENDS

WARREN SHUMWAY

Cover Photo: Casy Horner on Unsplash

Book and Cover Design: Hannah Wood

www.hannahwood.myportfolio.com

Dedicated to the woman of my dreams, Marina

1

Nathan

Ninety-six, ninety-seven, the muscles in my arms burn, ninety-eight, I love the burn, ninety-nine, one hundred. Push-ups done. I jump to my feet and start my squats. I do the first three slowly. On the fourth I start jumping a foot in the air after each one, landing deep into my next squat. The boat doesn't move. We haven't moved in three days. No wind, no waves, no movement. Nothing but the sun beating down on us. No sign of life other than my mom and dad getting it on in their cabin last night. We're somewhere between California and Hawaii on a custom-made sailboat Dad says is unsinkable. The ocean looks like a sheet of glass. Forty-five, forty-six, my quads are on fire. No land in sight. My lungs start to burn. I jump even higher after each squat. Fifty-five, fifty-six. How many more days of this? I should be with Mercedes, back in school, not stuck on a fifty-two foot sailboat with my parents. Sixty. I jump as high as I can on the last one and let out a scream. I catch my breath, take two steps toward the mast and grab hold of the main with both hands and start the first of three sets of fifty chin-ups.

I'm in good shape. Always have been. With parents like mine, you can't avoid it. A sedentary life isn't an option in our house. I'm eighteen, six feet, 170 lbs and have blond hair that has grown to my shoulders in the three months we've been on this trip. Mom's been calling me her surfer baby. A sport I'm looking forward to learning once we get to Hawaii. Though, I should probably cut my hair first so I don't get ragged on too much by the locals. Nothing worse than looking like an expert in something when you actually suck. Forty-eight, Forty-nine. On my last chin-up of the first set I do a backward somersault between my arms and lock my feet around the mast. Hanging upside down I do fifty incline sit-ups. My stomach feels like lava. It's 5 am and the sunrise is spectacular. Rich reds cover the sun as it rises up. I flip back around to a chin-up position and do my second set; then I lay on deck and do one set of one hundred fifty leg lifts, then get back up and do my final set of chin-ups. My head stops racing. I love the calm that extreme workouts give me. I shut my eyes and do my first ten-minute meditation of the day. When I open them the sky has turned to an eerie mix of reds. *Red sky at night, sailors delight. Red sky in morning, sailors take warning* comes to mind.

"Dad. Mom. I think you need to come see this." I yell towards the cabin below.

2

Three months ago Dad asked, "What could be better than exploring the world on a boat?"

"Gee Dad, I don't know. Maybe the fact that I can't sit through a class without running three miles before, or because I'm seventeen and my hormones are through the roof, or because, for the first time in my life, I love school – I was actually loving school."

I have a lot of energy. I used to be hyper. Really hyper! Bouncing off walls hyper. Never tired hyper. Nonstop talking. Nonstop moving. Always on the go. I'd take on any dare or physical challenge. Race down the hallways. Scale the sides of the school buildings. Jump off the rooftops, until in fifth grade the school had had enough. The principal demanded my parents put me on medication to calm me down. I don't remember exactly what was said because my dad made me wait outside the office while he had a little chat with Mr. Voss. All I do remember was when Mom and Dad opened the door to leave the office I saw Mr. Voss's face was dark red and his eyes were all watery as if he might start to cry. He looked scared. Dad looked at me calmly and said, "Come on Son, we're going home." And home we went. And for the next four years my parents and others took turns and home-schooled me. Then, for my senior year, they sent me to a small private boarding school in the White Mountains of New Hampshire called Luke's Academy. It's the only school in the country that specializes in kids that are hyperactive or ADD, ADHD and dyslexic. I double qualified being both ADHD and dyslexic. Labels my mom and dad refuse to allow me to use as an excuse for doing anything poorly. Instead, they drilled into me that I had to excel in everything, because I was lucky to have the endless supply of energy ADHD gave me and just as lucky to have the creative mind that dyslexia gave me. They pushed me hard during my home-schooling years with some of the best outside help available in academics, computer coding, martial arts, first aid and outdoor survival skills. I excelled at everything after years of failure. I was never bored and loved the daily challenges that were set out for me; but I missed being around kids my own age. So when I got to Luke's Academy I was happy to be back in school and I enjoyed the boarding school life.

The day before my mom and dad set off on their trip around the world they came to see me and say goodbye. I was headed up to the gym roof to meditate and exercise before my last class, two things that were ingrained into my daily routine while I was home-schooled. Meditation and exercise are like brushing my teeth or going to the bathroom. I never miss a day.

So, I had walked out on the roof when I heard a muffled scream from behind the stairwell on the opposite side of the roof. I ran towards the stairwell and heard a guy yell "bitch", then heard a loud slap. Then a muffled cry. I ran as fast as I could, focused on the most direct route around the brick stairwell. My sneakers started to slip out from under me. The gravel that covered the tar rooftop was loose and I felt like a car power sliding around a corner. I increased my speed and barely made it around the corner without falling. Ten feet in front of me lay a half naked girl. Her underwear down around her left foot. Her toes and knees bloody. A guy naked from the waist down on top of her. His left hand was covered in blood and he had it over her mouth. His right hand was hidden below his waist. She turned her head in my direction. She looked like an injured animal in a PBS special that was getting attacked by a pack of wild boars. It was Mercedes. The girl I had just started dating.

I felt the rage as I dove towards them to attack. Time slowed. It felt like I was flying. I was focused on his left hand. That's the one I'd go for. I caught Mercedes' eye just before I landed on top of his back. The impact was harder than I expected. I could hear the wind get knocked out of Mercedes. But I landed where I wanted. My knees wrapped around his torso and I squeezed hard, stabilizing myself while at the same time I wrapped my left arm around his left elbow, putting him in an arm lock and then used my right hand to pull his elbow all the way back with everything I had. This wasn't a Jujitsu class. There would be no tapping out. I pulled until it snapped. His left shoulder, arm and wrist went limp in my hands. He screamed. Mercedes' eyes were wide open. She was trembling. I rolled off his back. He cried in pain. With his left arm hanging to his side he started to get to his knees. It was Chad, the all-star wide receiver for our football team, on his way to play ball at USC. "Let me explain," he said. I punched him hard in his left eye and then his right. Still on his knees, he fell back against the stairwell. It held him up. With everything I had I hit him one more time in each eye. I wanted to be sure his eyes were closed up so he would never again see Mercedes, who was now on her side crying. I stood up in front of him. His eyes were closing up. His body shook. I kicked him four times. Hard direct kicks to his balls. One perfectly placed kick after the other until he turned pale white and collapsed face first onto the gravel rooftop and started hyper-ventilating. I went to Mercedes and felt sick to my stomach seeing how banged up and scared she was. I knelt down, adjusted her skirt and picked her up when the stairwell doors flew open.

3

This trip around the world was Mom's idea. It was a dream she had since high school and my dad wanted to honor her dream while they were still young. But my dad being my dad, well, he had to design and build the safest and best high-tech sailboat possible. "An unsinkable boat," he told us. For the past two years Mom and Dad talked to me about how they were going to take off on a multi-year trip around the world while I went off on my own to explore opportunities and challenge myself as I saw fit.

We're wealthy, as you've probably figured out by now. My dad made his first million designing and patenting keyboards. Then he started a computer security business, which he turned into the most profitable Internet security business in the world. One of his longtime employees said to me, "your dad has a one hundred percent success rate when it comes to business." But dad laughed it off when I told him. "I failed my way to success. For every keyboard I designed, every application I developed, I had at least twenty that failed first. I'm just better about letting failure go then most. You have to be if you want to succeed Nathan. You don't succeed at anything unless you're willing to fail. Make failure fun. Failure is part of the overall process of success, so it's not a big deal when it happens. Fail. Tweak your moves. Fail. Tweak your attitude. Fail. Adjust. And move ahead. That's how you succeed."

His security business has given us a net worth of over two billion dollars. Half of it in cash, which is spread out in banks, safe deposit boxes and hidden safes on our properties; the other half is invested in the stock market. He's self-made and says anything in life is possible and he uses himself as an ongoing example. "Doesn't matter if you want to be a doctor, a professor, a CEO, a plumber or a professional athlete, Nathan. When you decide on something you want to do, you do it, and you give it a hundred percent until you've mastered it. If you can imagine it, you can achieve it. Always honor a dream and always do the next right thing towards realizing that dream," he'd say to me or anyone else that asked him for advice. He's a black belt in both Taekwondo and Brazilian Jujitsu. The *Wall Street Journal* says he's the only billionaire not afraid of a street fight. And I've seen him in a few. He's always defending the guy being taken advantage of. One night we drove through downtown Los Angeles on the way to the airport when he took on three gang members that were beating on a homeless man at a red light. The homeless man ended up in the back of our limo. We delayed our flight while Dad worked the phones, lining up and paying for a six-month rehab. An hour later we were all on our jet flying to Wisconsin instead of Westchester County to drop off Morgan, our new friend, at Rehab.

My mom is the magnetic field of the family, always guiding

my dad and me. Without her we'd be lost. She's an interior designer specializing in high-end homes and apartments; she has clients in Westchester County, New York City, Europe and China. When she's not traveling for work she's doing yoga, art or volunteer work. She and my dad met when she was a senior at Brown University, and Dad had just started his first business. They got married seven days after their fist date, and unlike my friends' parents my mom and dad still love each other and act like teenagers who just met for the first time.

4

The school dean and local police department decided I was at fault and locked me up in the town jail for the night. The next morning I was brought to the school security office to wait for my parents. They were coming up to take me to lunch and say goodbye before their adventure. Or so they thought. The dean was pissed that my parents didn't answer their cell phones when he called and couldn't understand my dad's theory of no communication for twenty-four hours once a week.

"How can your father run a business if people can't get in touch with him?" the dean snapped.

"Obviously pretty well," I said.

So we were sitting in the dean's office being told by the dean that I had violated school policy by using violence to settle an argument, that I would be expelled, and that I was facing criminal charges that could land me in jail. I had given my parents the two-minute version of what happened while we walked from the campus security office to the dean's office. Mom put her arm around me when I told them about Mercedes. Dad said nothing. The dean went over his version of the events. Then he went into great detail about what a good student Chad was. When he finished speaking, my father just stared at him. He didn't say a word. He just looked directly into the dean's eyes for what seemed like a really long time. It was uncomfortable. The dean broke first.

"This is serious, Jack," the dean said.

Dad kept his stare going. "Tell me more about Chad," Dad said.

"Excuse me," the dean said, looking away from my dad towards the wall.

"Chad. Tell me more about Chad. What other kind of trouble has he been in?"

"Chad's still in the hospital. His mother is flying in later today to be at his side. The police didn't find any marks, scratches, or any sign of entry. The girl was there on her own free will and your son in a jealous rage blind-sided and attacked Chad."

"My question," Dad said in a low voice, "was what other kind of trouble has Chad been in?"

"He, ah…," I started to say.

"Stop," Dad said to me.

"Chad's been an A student both in class and on the football field. He's been a role model for the other students and he's well liked by staff and students alike," the dean said.

Dad turned to me and shook his head with disappointment. "I'm sorry to hear that, dean," he said.

I couldn't believe it. Dad didn't believe me. I never lie to my parents. There was never a need to. We have always been open about everything. My entire home-schooling experience was based on honest communication. Nothing was ever held back.

The dean took Dad's disappointment as an opening and said, "Look Jack, clearly you're upset. I would be too. This is tough for you, Julie, the Academy, Chad's family, and especially for Chad. Let's just hope for Nathan's sake Chad's football career isn't over. We've been real lucky to keep this out of the mainstream media. No one wants their kid to be in this kind of trouble. I have an idea. I'll tell you what I'll do. We're building a new library at the Academy. Perhaps with a sizable donation on your part for the library and a settlement for Chad's family I can get Chad's parents and the police to drop the charges. I can't promise, but if the donation covers the entire project I might be able to do it for you."

Dad turned to Mom, then to the dean. And, without looking at me, said, "Thank you, dean. I'll need ten minutes on a computer and another five to call my accountant. Can you get me on a computer with some privacy and a printer so I can access an account?"

The dean fought off a smile that turned into a smirk. My mom looked down at the floor. She too? I couldn't believe it. How could they not trust me? This is crazy.

"Let me show you to a private office," the dean said, leaving Mom and me alone.

"Mom, this is crazy," I said.

"Nathan. Please," Mom said, putting a finger to her lips to silence me.

A minute later the dean came back into the office, happy as can be, with a catalog that he handed to Mom. It was loaded with photos and designs for the new library. "Take a look at this while I catch up on some work. It's an exciting project. The board is really excited about it," he said as he hit a few keys on his keyboard. Then he hit a few more. "Hate when these things freeze up," he said and reached around the back of the computer to shut if off.

After what seemed like an eternity, his computer was back on and he was typing away.

"What the hell?" he said and reached back a second time to restart the computer just as my dad walked into the office.

"Didn't take as long as I thought," Dad said and dropped a bunch of 8½" x 11" copies on the dean's desk.

"Fantastic!" the dean said.

"Read those," Dad said.

"What are they?"

"I think you'll figure it out," Dad said.

Mom looked at me. I looked at the dean. His demeanor changed pretty quickly as he read. His jaw and facial muscles tightened after the first page. When he finished the second page, he put the rest of the papers down and looked up in disbelief.

"This is what's going to happen," Dad said. "You are going to tell Chad's parents the truth. You and Chad are going to apologize to that girl. You are going to pick up that phone and call the police chief and tell him that if all charges aren't dropped against my son immediately this information is going to every major news network in the country. And if Chad is allowed back into this school this information is going public. If Chad doesn't get counseling this information goes public. And if this school doesn't ban this so-called Senior Mentor Day, this information goes public and this Academy is done." The dean looked like a deer caught in headlights. His mouth hung open in disbelief.

"Let Chad's family know that if Chad ever plays football again, anywhere, anytime or is involved with football in any way, this information goes public. The courts may not be able to prosecute him with the evidence, but we can. Call the chief."

The dean was frozen.

"Now!"

The dean picked up the phone and punched in a number. "Henry. Drop all charges on Nathan Paddington," he said and then listened to whatever the chief was saying. "Henry. Just do it. Drop them all. And drop them now. No, you don't need to come over. We have a problem, Henry. A real God damn problem!"

"Give me the phone," Dad said.

The dean handed the phone over immediately.

"Henry, this is Jack Paddington, Nathan's dad. My guess is you didn't want to get dragged into this mess, but with the school paying most of the town's taxes you feel you have to be loyal. I've got copies of the emails between you and the dean discussing Chad's involvement with the other six girls. How all six of those girls' GPA went from 2.5 to 4.0 after they dropped their complaints against Chad," Dad said. "No, Henry. Nothing is private on the Internet. Unless you drop all these charges now, and I mean within the next five minutes, this information goes national and you'll be working the door at Walmart." Dad listened for a beat. "No. I have no interest in meeting you. You have five minutes." A beat. "No, it's not a threat. I don't make threats, Henry. Never have. Never will. I make promises. Promises I keep. Copy me and my lawyer on all of the dropped charges. You have five minutes from the time I hang up this phone." Dad gave him both email addresses and said again, "Five minutes, Henry. The clock starts now." Dad hung up the phone and sat next to Mom. She put her hand on his lap as he turned to me. "Good job, Son," he said softly. I almost burst into tears.

Five and a half minutes later we walked out of the dean's office with a copy of the email from the police chief saying all charges had been dropped. Dad didn't smile, didn't shake the dean's hand and didn't say another word to him as we walked out of the office.

5

We carried the last of my stuff from the dorm to the car.
I hadn't said goodbye to any of my friends or even talked to
anyone other than the police and the dean since yesterday.
Being locked up will do that. I got my cell phone and wallet
back from the security office and texted Mercedes. The campus
was empty and would be for a few more minutes.

What was she thinking? He's nothing like her. He's an ego-
tistical prick. She has nothing in common with him. Why
would she even go up to the rooftop with him? She is ... she
was ... my girlfriend.

"You did the right thing," Mom said, breaking me away from
my thoughts.

"Thanks," I said.

The bell went off, signaling the end of classes, and all the
doors flew open as if synchronized. Most of the kids walked out
looking at their cell phones. Some ran to beat the lunch line. A
few couples held hands. Tera, Sara, and Brea, the hottest girls

at Luke's according to our school paper, walked up to me and my parents.

"Hey, Nathan," Sara said. Yesterday, these girls didn't even know I existed. They're not my style. Chad's group is their style.

"You suspended?" Tera asked.

"That's bullshit, if you are," Sara said.

"Totally," Brea said. All three of them bordering on anorexia and dressed like they're on the red carpet.

"I'm all done here," I told them.

"He's leaving school to do some traveling with us," Mom said.

"I am?" I said, looking at Mom.

"Rad," Sara said. "Private plane?"

"Sailing," Mom said.

"Eh. Bummer," Sara said. I wasn't sure if she meant the sailing part or the fact that my mom grabbed my hand.

I saw Mercedes and we made quick eye contact. She lowered her head. "I gotta go," I said, letting go of Mom's hand. I jogged over to Mercedes, leaving Mom to deal with three of the richest girls in school who thought they were God's gift to the world, preferring to be with the girl on a full scholarship who bought her clothes at Goodwill or made them herself. Mercedes is an art student. She is super-talented. And super nice. She doesn't work at being beautiful. Mercedes is beautiful. She has ivory skin, strawberry-blond hair and crystal clear green eyes. She's stunning.

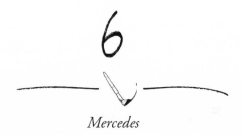

6

Mercedes

Oh, god, there's Nathan. I'm not ready to see him. How could he ever forgive me? I'm so stupid! What was I thinking? Chad, like Chad would really help me. See, Chad had asked Brea, to ask my roommate Melinda, to ask me, to meet up with Chad outside the auditorium. He had been recruited by USC on a full scholarship to play football and wanted to talk to me about selling my artwork to some of the galleries in Los Angeles for extra cash. I was so stupid. Melinda gave him my number. He texted me a photo of my work that is up in the school cafeteria, saying my paintings would do really well in L.A. He said he could get a thousand dollars for each painting. A thousand dollars is a lot of money, so I met him in the quad. He was drinking a grape-flavored Vita water and handed me a lemon flavored one that he opened for me. He was holding a pad of paper.

"Let's go up on the rooftop for some privacy so we can go over the paperwork," he said.

I couldn't believe it. Chad, the football star, is seriously going to go out and market my artwork. He's actually serious. So cool I thought. I took a drink of the Vita water and we walked up the two flights to the rooftop. I was tired from a long night of studying and felt a little dehydrated, so I took a large gulp of the Vita Water as Chad pushed open the door to the rooftop.

"After you," he said.

I walked out past him. "Thanks," I said smiling. *How did I get so lucky to have this guy, a football star, wanting to help sell my work?* I couldn't wait to tell Nathan.

"To successful art sales!" he toasted.

The door shut behind us with a loud thump. My vision started to blur. My legs got heavy. My body was giving out but my mind was present. "Chad. I don't feel so well," I said and looked back towards him. He had a big smile on his face. A real cocky smile.

"Welcome to Senior Mentor Day," he said.

My legs gave out and he watched me fall on the gravel rooftop. He was still smiling. Oh my god was all I could think. What the hell is happening? He drugged me? I was on my back. I looked up. Chad was grinning.

"This is going to push me to the top. Eight in a week. Baby, I win."

I had to get up and run. I tried. But I couldn't move. This can't be happening. I had to do something. I opened my mouth to scream but I had trouble even getting it open. He dove on me and covered my mouth like he was catching a football. He was fast. He kept one hand over my mouth and pulled his pants down with the other. Then he reached up under my skirt and ripped my underwear off. No. Please God. Please don't let this be happening. I could feel his erection pressed against me. It felt like a weapon. One of his fingers slipped into my mouth. I begged for the strength to close my mouth, and I bit down as hard as I could.

"Ahhhh," he yelled and slapped me across the face. "Just take it bitch! Artists love to fuck," he said and tried to push into me as I willed my legs closed. "Come on," he said and spit into his hand and then reached down.

Oh my god. This was going to happen. He was going to rape me. He pushed his thumb into my vagina. I turned my head to close myself off from the world. I saw Nathan, the kid who smiled and talked to me when everyone else just walked by. We had just started texting each other and were planning on getting together on Saturday night for our first date. I saw him by the door. Am I hallucinating? No. I actually saw Nathan. By the far door. Yes, there he is again. I caught his eye. Now he's gone. I thought maybe I was dreaming. Maybe this whole thing was just a really bad dream. That calmed me a bit. Yes. A dream. Lets just say this was a really bad dream.

Then I heard a high-pitched scream coming from Chad that brought me back to reality. Nathan pulled up my underwear. He asked if I was all right. He kissed me on the forehead. A tear fell from his eye onto my cheek. He lifted me up off the ground. Chad was on his side hyperventilating and crying. I remember having my arms around Nathan's neck when doors to the rooftop flew open. And I remember the security cop and two teachers running towards us. But that's it. I passed out.

7

When I woke up I was in a hospital bed. A needle in my arm was attached to a clear plastic tube that came from a bag above the bed. I was dressed in a hospital gown. It was pushed up above my waist. A woman and a man were hunched over and looking between my legs. Something cold was inside of me. A male police officer stood against the wall of the room. Two other men were in the room. They were all looking. I shut my eyes, not wanting them to know I was awake.

"Chad's not going to be able to play ball for at least a year. Maybe never. That kid did some serious damage," one man said.

"Think USC will still take him?" another man asked.

"No forced entry. No penetration," the male doctor said.

"There's your answer. Yeah, they'll take him," the other man said.

"Bruises to her thighs, stomach and lower buttocks that fit a rape attempt," the female doctor said.

"How do you know that?" another male asked.

"The bruises are from the head of a penis, officer," the male doctor said.

"The whole thing could be a set-up. Maybe she was going to blackmail him," the cop said.

"Get out. All of you get out," ordered the female doctor.

I was back in my dorm room by 8:30 last night. My roommate asked me what happened to Chad. I told her I had no idea and took one of the pills the nurse had given me and went to sleep.

Now I had to face reality. Nathan loved this school so much. He loved being in New Hampshire too. He's not like most of the other kids. He's not like any kid I've ever met before. He's so open and honest about his feelings. He knows who he is. He loves art, he loves to explore, he loves to learn even though it's hard for him to read, he loves conversation. How was I ever going to apologize to him? To his mom and dad? I had to do it. I had to let them know how sorry I am.

8

Nathan

"Hey," I said.

"Hey," she said, holding back a tear.

I wanted to ask her what she was doing with Chad on the roof. I was pissed before, but all I really cared about was that she was okay.

"Those girls. The ones you were talking to.

"Yeah," I said.

"They set it up".

"Set what up?" I asked.

"Everything. They told me to meet up with Chad. Brea said he had chosen me for Senior Mentor Day. He wanted to help get my art in some of the galleries in Los Angeles. He said he wanted to mentor me." Tears started to escape from her green eyes. Her breathing grew deeper. She looked down. Trying to hold it together. "I'm so stupid. I didn't know Senior Mentor Day was for hook-ups. I believed them. Nathan. If…if…if you

31

hadn't come up, he would have….." She sobbed and wrapped her arms around me. I hugged her back. "Thank you," she said and squeezed me harder.

Our first hug, great; now the girl I'm falling in love with is hugging me and what am I going to do? I'm going to go on a frigging sailboat with my mom and dad for a year.

"Come on. I want you to meet my parents," I said.

She looked up, her eyes still full of tears, but she had stopped crying. "Like this? I don't think so," she said with a hint of a smile. My god, her smile makes me melt.

I held her hand, it was soft, warm and it molded into mine. The connection was electric. I felt my body temperature rise. My skin tingled. "Come on," I said and pulled her towards my parents.

Mom and Dad were leaning against our old Toyota Land Cruiser. A car my dad would tell all his young employees was paid for in full and that if American families bought their cars in cash the savings they would get from not paying interest, if invested properly, could total a hundred thousand dollars. "Just because you have money, doesn't mean you should waste it," he'd say. Meanwhile, he has three Ferrari racecars, a private jet and two single-engine planes, one off each coast.

"Mom, Dad, this is Mercedes," I said.

"Hi, Mrs. and Mr. Paddington. Nice to meet you," Mercedes said.

"Please call me Julie."

"And I'm Jack."

"I'm so sorry," Mercedes said.

"How are you, sweetie?" Mom asked.

"I'm okay". Mercedes whispered back.

Mom opened her arms and, as if by some kind of magnetic force, Mercedes took two steps forward as Mom wrapped her arms around her in a hug. Mercedes started to cry. Mom turned her head towards Dad and me. Her look said it all. We'd seen that look plenty of times before. Someone needed help and Mom needed her space.

"What do you say we run that two-mile loop of yours," Dad said as we walked away from Mom and Mercedes.

"Three-mile loop. Think you can handle it?"

We both had sneakers on. Dad always told me, don't make exercise a big deal. You don't have to go to a gym or change clothes for every workout. You don't have to have the latest equipment. You just have to do it. Wear running sneakers as often as you can so you're always ready. There's no excuse for being out of shape, he'd preach.

I looked over at Mom and Mercedes. They were sitting side by side at the picnic table holding hands.

So Dad, in his faded jeans and V-neck short-sleeve polo shirt, and me in cutoff shorts and a T-shirt, we took off running. The first mile was through a thick pine forest with two good hills. We ran side by side at a six-minute pace. The next mile flattened out and we ran faster along the river. The kayak team was practicing wind sprints. We raced them until our trail veered left, deeper into the woods and up a steep hill. Dad passed me.

"Come on Nate. Push it." He yelled.

I passed him at the crest of the hill and then turned around running backwards.

"What was that?" I asked.

Dad smiled. My foot went into a puddle and I fell backwards, hitting the ground hard and losing a sneaker.

"Don't get cocky," Dad said running past me without asking if I was all right. He was a good fifty yards in front of me by the time I got my shoe back on. I ran as fast as I could. The finish line, our car, was two football fields away. I was a better sprinter and I was gaining on him. My lungs burned. Fifty feet from catching him, twenty, ten, five, two, one, we were side by side. I ran faster. He matched my pace. I ran even faster. He fell back a stride and exhaled quickly and deeply three times. Then he ran past me and sprinted the last twenty feet, beating me to the car by a stride. We both collapsed on the ground, panting and laughing.

"I love you," I said laughing.

"Love you back, kid."

After we caught our breath, we headed over to the now empty picnic table where I had seen Mercedes and Mom sitting when we left. Dad sat down first with his legs away from the table and began to stretch.

"You shouldn't have kicked him," Dad said. "If those emails didn't exist, you would be in a lot of legal trouble. As it is, his parents could still sue with a good lawyer."

"I know, Dad. I thought I was too late. I thought Chad had been inside her. I didn't want him to be able to have any kind of sex again," I said.

"Always control your emotions. Deep breaths. Even in the heat of battle, Nathan," he said and put his arm over my shoulder.

9

Nathan

Mercedes and Mom walked out of the cafeteria building. Mom had her arm over Mercedes' shoulder and was talking as she pointed to me and Dad. Mercedes was smiling, then started laughing at whatever my mom said. You could feel genuine admiration between them as they walked to the table. Dad and I stood up. "Thank you so much," Mercedes said.

"You're welcome. And thank you. I've never met an undiscovered artist with so much talent. Remember, stay in touch. We'll have Internet access on the boat. Email or call when you need anything," Mom said and then turned to Dad. "Let's give them a few minutes to say goodbye," she said.

I walked closer to Mercedes. "Hey," I said.

"Hey," she said. "Wish I had a mom like yours."

"She's pretty cool for a mom," I said.

Mercedes stared into my eyes. Her eyes. Her eyes. I love her eyes.

"Nathan," she said.

"Yes," I said, snapping out of it.

"Thank you," she said and leaned in and kissed me gently on the lips.

10

Half an hour later I was in the car with my mom and dad driving farther and farther away from the girl I was in love with and the school I enjoyed. We drove in silence, all of us comprehending the chain of events that had just occurred.

When we got into Connecticut, Dad turned away from the road and handed me a spiral note pad. "Here, even though you're going with us, I still want you to memorize these two pages." He turned back to the road. "I've been a pretty good dad. Taught you what I think are skills in order for you to survive in this world. But some things we haven't discussed yet, because I felt you were too young. Not ready. I set up a bunch of audio and video clips on a secure address for you to watch in case something happened to your mom and me. Memorize those two pages, Nathan," he said.

"But I am going with you, so why bother?" I asked.

Mom and Dad gave each other a look I hadn't seen before.

"I am going, right?"

"Yes, Nathan," Mom said. "But, I talked to your dad about it while you were saying goodbye to Mercedes. We think you should only go as far as Hawaii. If Mercedes' parents are okay with it, we could fly her out and you two could spend a summer there or you could fly back and live or explore wherever you'd like. That girl has such a beautiful soul, Nathan, and I can tell she cares for you as much as you care for her."

"Nathan," my dad said. "The trip your mom and I planned is pretty extreme. As you know, we plan to be away for a few years. We're going to be sailing through some pretty sketchy areas. I've taken all the necessary precautions but stuff happens. Pirates happen. Storms happen. The point I'm trying to make is this: your mom and I have spent the past few years preparing you to live a life without us in case something ever happened to us," he said.

"Yeah, yeah. I know. I'm an only child. No grandparents. No cousins. Only distant relatives we don't know. I got it. But you're going to be fine. You always are."

Dad looked over at Mom. "I want you to have those pages memorized by tomorrow morning," he said.

The pages were full of property locations, URLs, and information on two-dozen banks scattered around the country. "This is your investment information," I said.

"It's just some savings information. Cash locations. Enough money for you, and your family, should you decide to have one, to live on."

"Just be smart with it," Mom said.

"You sound like you're planning to disappear," I said as Mom smiled at Dad.

"Money is a positive, Nate. Make it work for you. Have fun with it. Help others with it. But don't waste it and don't give it away unless you get something in return.

Dad and Mom always talked about life on earth and how we have to make the most of it. They talked about how our journeys continue after this life. They were always preparing me in case something happened to them. They did do a lot of international travel and Mom's parents died in a car accident and Dad's mom died when he was a kid and he never met his father. And since neither had any siblings, I have no grandparents and no cousins. They were always preparing me for life without them.

I went back to the list Dad gave me and, using a memorization technique I learned at Luke's, I chunked it down and started with the land locations. By the time we pulled into our driveway I had the list memorized.

Mercedes

Nathan's mom and dad were amazing. No wonder he's such a great kid. How could he not be with parents like that? I felt as much love in my heart for them as I did for Nathan. But my love for Nathan was different; that love I felt throughout my body. Being close to Nathan gives me feelings I haven't had before. I've never kissed a boy first. The boys have always kissed me first and they've always been drunk. And it's never been good. That's why I stopped dating. I got tired of guys just wanting to get it on. I wanted more. I wanted an intimate experience. There was no way I was going to lose my virginity to those guys. Sure, I let some of them touch me or kiss me down there. And I did the same to some of them, but I got tired of the games the guys played, so I stopped dating and focused on my artwork. I don't know why I kissed Nathan. All I know is that when our lips touched my body came alive and fire filled my veins. I wanted him so badly.

I watched as the Paddingtons' car drove down the dirt road and disappeared as it rounded the corner. Nathan's dad wanted to drive out the academy's back road that was for emergencies only. It's an unmaintained dirt road that's full of potholes and runs through a swamp. If they don't get stuck it will take them to the base of Mount Washington. I watched as the dust from their tires settled back down to the ground. I was so blessed to have met this family. I looked into the sky and said a quick prayer of thanks for bringing Nathan into my life and headed back to my dorm.

That's when things got weird.

12

I had decided to skip my last class and paint while the visual of the White Mountains towering over the Paddingtons' Land Cruiser was fresh in my mind. I turned to leave God's self portrait when I saw him – he stood out like an FBI agent in a bad film. Patagonia, Northface and Mountain Hardware jackets are the norm for men here. This guy was dressed in a black tailored suit. He had black shoes that looked new and he had a buzz cut. He also had a camera that was pointed at me. Last night came rushing back to me. I looked right at him, thinking he would put the camera down. But he didn't. Instead, he grabbed the lens and twisted it while snapping photos. I gave him the finger and felt sick to my stomach. It brought me back to the rooftop, filling me with anxiety.

Outside my dorm I saw Melinda carrying boxes down the stairs with a man dressed exactly like the guy taking pictures. They loaded the boxes into a black van.

"Melinda," I tried to yell, but my anxiety wouldn't allow it. She got into the van without looking and the man dressed in black shut the door.

I walked into my room and two more men dressed in black were there. One was cleaning the floor with a broom, the other was putting drawers back into my dresser. "What, what, what are you doing with my clothes? With my things?" I asked, feeling like I might faint.

"We thought it was Melinda's stuff, but it's not." He said without offering an apology.

"Get out," I ordered as best as I could.

They walked out leaving me in a room that was now half bare. I wasn't close to Melinda. We had nothing in common other than that we were the only two girls on full scholarships: mine for art, hers for field hockey. Why did she leave? Who are those men? I didn't like having a roommate. In fact, I craved privacy, but now that I had it the empty space scared me.

"Be strong Mercedes," I told myself.

My head was about to explode. I've had some anxiety but this was scary. This felt like I was about to lose my mind. My brain was bouncing off the walls of my skull – my vision started to blur. "Oh God. I'm going crazy – help me," I said out loud to myself. Create something – anything that will get rid of my anxiety. Good. That's what I'll do.

I left my room and headed for the art department. The quad was full of students that parted, leaving a wide path for me to walk. "Rat" someone yelled out. Then another "Rat", then a few more until the entire quad was chanting "Rat, rat, rat, rat". A lot of them had their phones pointed at me as they chanted. Rat, rat, rat, Mercedes is a rat. Rat, rat, rat, rat, Mercedes is a rat.

I'm not sure why, but for some reason, their chanting gave me strength – it cleared my anxiety. I was empowered by their hatred and immaturity. I stood up tall, thanked them and walked calmly to the art department where I took the anxiety that had fueled my head, the experience on the rooftop and the visual of Nathan and his family driving towards the White Mountains and put it onto canvas.

Six hours later I was done. Mr. Fleming, an artist from upstate N.Y, and our teacher for the year, was working on a piece himself when I walked in - we made eye contact, he nodded his head and then went back to his work. He was a good man, an incredible artist that didn't need to teach. I had forgotten he was in the room. I had forgotten I was in the room. I painted not knowing new blisters were forming on my hand, not knowing it was past midnight, not knowing anything except the canvas that lay in front of me that was now done.

"My God," Mr. Fleming said.

I turned to face him. He had tears in his eyes.

"Mercedes," he said, but nothings else.

"I don't care if it's not any good, Mr. Fleming, it helped me."

"No Mercedes. No, it's not good. It's, magnificent – powerful – beautiful. It's some of the best work I've ever seen," he said.

13

Nathan— Sailboat

Dad stayed up most of the night downloading and copying files to thumb drives. He connected to a Russian satellite and found information on American CEOs, politicians, celebrities and professional athletes. Information that none of them would want to be made public. I walked into the cabin that he uses as an office as he was downloading a photo of Senator Grant in bed with two young Thai boys. All of them were naked. For a second I got scared. Was he looking at porn? Child porn?

"What are you looking at, Dad?" I ask.

"Nate. What are you doing here? You should be asleep."

"I couldn't sleep. I came to get a battery charger."

He looked a little nervous. Rushed. Something I've never seen in my dad. He looked away from me and back at the computer, and said, "The Russians own everyone in these photos, Nate. This is blackmail material that could change the direction of America. These photos have the power to decide who our next president will be. What laws will be passed. Who will win the next Super Bowl."

"What are you going to do with it?" I ask.

"I don't know. This changes everything, or nothing, Nathan. Depending on what we do with it. We do the right thing, our lives will never be the same. We would lose everything. Including our lives. If we do nothing, well, then we would have to live with ourselves, knowing we did nothing," he says, staring at me.

"Dad."

He looked at me as if he hadn't seen me in months. "Nathan. Sometimes in life, you have to give up what you love most, leave everything you love behind in order to do what's right."

"Come on, Dad. It's not that bad."

"Yes. It is." He says.

"Why don't you email the information to the New York *Times* or snail mail it when we get to the next port?"

"The Times wouldn't go near this. Their own CEO is listed and photographed. Along with the *Wall Street Journal, LA Times and Washington Post*. They have information on almost all American senators, both democrats and republicans, CNN and Fox. The Russians have America wrapped around their fingers," he says.

"So let's set up a Snapchat or Facebook account and send the information out that way," I say.

My dad can set up accounts for people that would never be found. That's how he made his money. So he could do it if he really wanted to.

"One wrong move, Nate, and we'd have to face the KGB, the CIA, the FBI, and a bunch of black ops that don't have initials and don't make arrests. We'd have to live off the grid for the remainder of our lives. If we got caught with this information we would be shot or put away somewhere that doesn't have an address."

When I left his cabin at 3 am he was still downloading onto thumb drives.

14

For the first time in my life, my dad isn't up before me. I look back at the red sky and yell this time. "Mom. Dad. You really need to see this now. I think we're in trouble."

Dad walks up on deck, wearing an old pair of sweat pants and nothing else. He's still ripped with an upper body that looks more like a professional athlete or model then a CEO.

"Wow," Dad says, not looking surprised.

"Is it true, the red sky in the morning sailors take warning?" I ask.

"Afraid so," he says, walking back below deck.

I take a picture of the sunrise with my cell phone and email it to Mercedes. We'd been FaceTiming every day. She left school because she felt ostracized by the staff and other students and is living back home with her dad and stepmom and finishing her senior year at a public school. Her dad is a drunk and walked into her room when we were FaceTiming last night. He had a 24-oz can of Miller and said to her, "Why didn't you just screw the guy and get pregnant like any other girl would do? God knows you've screwed before. Why not him? You would have been set for life. The kid's on his way to the NFL Now what do you get? Ha?"

Mercedes had made me promise I wouldn't tell Mom that she left school. She didn't want to spoil Mom's dream vacation. But this, this I wasn't okay with and I wouldn't leave it alone. Mercedes still doesn't know how rich we are. I decided to ask Mom and Dad if we could send her to another private school. My plan is to pitch the idea tonight at dinner.

My phone vibrates, Mercedes's smile pops up on FaceTime.

"Hey," I say.

"Hey, it's so beautiful."

"Check this out." I move the phone away from me and pan the horizon. "Think you can paint it?"

"Just need some oils," she says. "The funding for art class was cut. Hey, I dreamed about you last night," she says.

I love her puffy eyes in the morning.

"What happened?" I asked

She leans back. Her T-shirt lifted a bit exposing her waistline. She giggles. My body tingles.

"Nathan. I'm going to need some help," Dad yells from below.

I look into Mercedes' green eyes that are thousands of miles away. "Looks like we have a storm coming," I say.

Mercedes' expression changes. "Be careful."

"Of course," I say.

"Hey. I … eh," she says.

"Nathan, move!" Dad yells.

"I'll call tonight or tomorrow, depending on how bad it is," I say.

"Now Nathan!" Dad yells.

"Gotta go. I love you". I say ending the call before she can respond. I said it! I meant it. I love her.

15

The swells have been steady at six feet. The wind is at 40 knots. Dad spent the past six hours alternating between the radio, the Internet and the weather channel. They were warning about severe hurricane conditions. He decided we would head east and try to out-run the storm.

"You still glad we went off course to connect to that satellite?" Mom asks.

"Wish I'd been wrong about it," he says.

"Jesus, Jack. Are we really going public with this?"

"Putin's got our president and the mainstream media in his pocket. What do you think we should do?" he asks Mom.

"Finish our trip." She says looking at him. "Let it go until then"

"And I'm so good at letting things go." Dad says sarcastically.

"Hey," I say, pointing to the sky behind us that was now solid black. No light at all. A sheer black wall that looks like the end of the earth and it's moving fast towards us. The three of us stand as if frozen in place staring. The boat rolls over the waves.

"To the chairs." Dad screams. Then, more to himself, he yells, "Windows, hatch, lock us in! Windows, hatch, lock us in!" And he keeps repeating it while he starts to accomplish all three.

I pull out my cell and snap a quick photo of the black wall closing in on us and send it to Mercedes. Then I follow Mom into the cabin and we strap ourselves into the chairs that my dad had custom built. The boat starts to rise at a faster pace. The swells are getting bigger. What is taking Dad so long?

The boat takes a violent turn and then drops off a wave sideways. We hit hard. Dad runs into the main cabin, bouncing off the walls past me and Mom. He grabs the custom air-lock wheel that is attached to the cabin door and turns it left as fast as he can, sealing us in. The cabin gets eerily quiet. I check my safety belts to make sure they are snug. Dad pushes a button on the control panel that is built into the left armrest of his chair and that powers the navigation system for the boat. He can now steer and control the speed of the boat from the electronic panel and monitor.

He reaches up above his head and turns on the oxygen tanks. A flashing red light followed by a loud beep let us know the oxygen is on and working. Mom's seat is directly across from Dad's, so they could have eye contact if they needed to use the seats. My seat was a last-minute addition and is off to my dad's right. Dad said that once the hatch and windows are locked down tight you could roll over in the boat all night long without sinking. It's airtight.

Seasickness is another issue though. We have been locked

in for only a few minutes and my stomach is not adjusting. I look over at Mom. She has a smile on her face but I can tell she is feeling it too. "First one to get sick cleans the boat after the storm," she says.

The black wall races past us. One second I'm looking at Mom and the next I can't see anything. Blackness. The sound of baseballs being thrown at the boat is deafening. "Must be hail," Mom yells. The control lights on the navigation grow brighter and I can see Mom's shadow. Dad's seat is empty.

16

The waves grow massive.

"Dad," I yell. The boat turns quickly to the port side and sends us crashing into the side of the next wave. Dad's shadow comes flying back into the main cabin and smashes into the fridge. He grunts in pain.

"Sorry about that," Dad says, crawling to his seat.

"Hurry sweetie," Mom yells.

Dad straps himself in and I can see his face from the reflection of the panel lights. The boat goes sideways again and we rise higher and higher. Dad pushes a few more buttons and the roar of the engine grows louder than the hail. I can feel the boat turning on the crest of a wave.

"It's now or never," Dad yells. The engine screams louder and louder, sounding like it is going to blow any second. Time stands still as we teeter on top of the wave.

And now, we are surfing with the waves instead of crashing sideways into them. "This could get interesting," Dad says.

With each wave growing larger then the previous one, our speed increases down the backside of each wave, pushing our bow deeper and deeper into the ocean until it finally goes completely under water, stopping us as another wave comes crashing down on us and spinning us around.

Dad works the controls and somehow gets us straightened out. We rise. We surf. We rise. We surf. Incredibly, each wave is still growing larger.

"I know I said it before, but this time it's really now or never," Dad yells. "We're going to head into it. Hold on," he screams.

"Are you sure?" Mom asks.

"She's unsinkable, but a few more hits like that could rip off the mast," he says.

We ride up the top of the next wave. "Here we go," he yells. The engine screams again, fighting the force of the ocean's power and sounding like it is going to explode. Somehow we do a one-eighty and are climbing the waves headed directly into the storm. It feels like we are driving up a hill that is almost vertical. At the top of each wave we go airborne and smack down on the back side of it. Even with the cushioned seats, each landing is jarring on our backs. We aren't surfing anymore.

"Well this sucks," I yell.

"Yes. But the waves aren't crashing on top of us," Dad yells back.

Mom starts to say something but pukes instead.

"Breathe, honey," Dad says. The second I get a whiff of Mom's puke I get sick too. One after another we both throw up.

The boat keeps climbing higher and higher and crashing down harder and harder each time. It feels like we are going to flip over backwards. The bow keeps rising, and instead of reaching the peak of the wave and crashing back down like we'd been doing so many times, we keep climbing. "We're vertical", I yell.

Everything slows down as the bow is pushed to the point of no return. I can feel that we are airborne flipping over backwards. I'm upside down pressed up against the seat belts. We hit hard. The boat stops for a brief second, leaving us at the mercy of the ocean. The next wave crashes down onto us with all its force and sends us into an upside down spin. Silence. Not a sound. No hail. No rain. No engine. We are under the surface of the ocean. How deep, I have no idea. Mom moans.

"We're good," Dad says. But his voice is raw and for the first time in my life it lacks confidence. We pop back out from under the ocean, and instantly get hit by another wave that sends us back under. We pop out faster this time, but something is different.

"We've lost power," Dad yells. With no engine, we don't have any way to steer the boat and we roll again. It feels like we're in a washing machine or an out-of-control amusement park ride. When I first sat in this seat, the cushioning was comfortable, it felt like I was at an Imax theater; now it feels like concrete that my head is being hammered against.

"Sorry about this," Mom yells.

"We'll be laughing about this tomorrow," I yell.

Dad pukes. We are lifted back up and into another backwards somersault and get pushed sideways on the landing. Another wave hits us full force. My eardrums feel like they are going to explode. A loud cracking sound comes from directly behind my head. Something hard is hitting the side of the boat. We roll again, and when we come back up whatever hit us before hits us again, but this time it hits the window to my right, cracking it.

The black wall has passed us, leaving a grey sky that gives us some light. The worst of the storm has passed us. We are all covered in vomit. Mom and Dad are as white as ghosts. I'm sure I am the same.

We roll again. "The boat may be unsinkable, but whatever is hitting us is about to put a hole through the side," Dad yells.

We ride up a wave that seems smaller then the others, but crashes down just as hard. Each wave we hit is followed up with what sounds like a hammer smashing into us. And this time it hits directly behind my head. The crack is loud enough for us all to hear.

"Jack," Mom yells.

"I see it, baby." Dad undoes his safety belt. He is pale but he has his confidence back, knowing he has to get us out of this situation. He takes one step out of his seat when we get hit by a wave that rolls us again. Dad hits the wall hard, and lands on the ceiling since we are upside down. We roll back around sending Dad back on the floor. He grabs hold of the stepladder as we ride up a smaller wave. The porthole to my side gets hit again, further cracking the unbreakable glass.

"It's the satellite," Dad yells. He grabs the safety kit under the stairs and pulls out a bolt cutter. We get hit again.

"I've got to cut it off."

"That's insane Jack," Mom yells.

"It's our only chance. If it hits the window again and we roll over, we're done. I'll tie in."

"Jack," Mom yells.

"Under no circumstances do you come out. Stay put," he screams, looking at both of us.

Dad turns the wheel on the door until it opens. He steps out and seals the door shut behind him. Mom and I look at each other. The sky is lighter. The rain is still coming down, but not as hard, and most of the waves seem to be getting smaller.

Most of my friends don't have close relationships with their parents. I do. I love my mom and dad as parents, mentors and friends. They're everything to me. Sure they embarrass me, piss me off sometimes, but they've always been there for me. "He'll be fine," Mom yells. "He always is." She manages a smile.

"I know," I say as we ride up a wave that keeps getting larger. The boat keeps rising with the wave. Mom is staring out my window. "Come on, Jack," she mouths the words. I turn my head as far to my right as I can. We continue rising with the wave. I can see Dad in his yellow rain slicker. He is leaning off the side of the boat, his arms stretched out holding the bolt cutters. We are almost vertical. Then we are. We flip over backwards like so many times before, but this time, Dad is outside.

We roll back up. I start to undo my safety harness. "No, Nathan," Mom yells.

I don't answer. I unclip the last buckle and I am in the air, stretched out going head first across the cabin. I see the handrail, that is my focus, it is at eye level. All I have to do is grab it.

"Nathan," Mom screams. Instinctively, I move my eyes away from the handrail towards her command - as I sail across the cabin. I feel a tingle in the back of my neck. I'm getting heavy. The black sky that was racing across the ocean to catch our boat is now racing to catch me – it does, and I'm out.

17

I'm in the academy's washing machine being tossed in circles with thousand of sheets, and rocks to help take out the stains. But why am I here? Why would I be in the washing machine? I can't figure it out. Am I dreaming? It hurts. Every time I roll with the clothes the rocks hit me in the face, my hips, knees and back. Water is going in and out of my ears. It's cold water. Why would anyone be washing sheets in cold water? Mom always said to wash sheets in warm or hot water.

I watch myself from the dream as I open my eyes. I'm lying in water. My body is shaking, and I'm rolling from one side of the cabin to the other. I'm awake. I'm on the boat. I look around. Mom and Dad must be outside. I sit up in the cold water. I'm shivering.

Something keeps hitting the bottom of the boat. The door to the outside is open. The port window is broken. The large waves are gone but the ocean is still angry, making the boat bounce in the rough choppy surface. Mom and Dad must be out organizing.

I walk out on deck. A fin glides toward the boat and at the last second disappears below the water's surface. More fins. Three, four, five fins and they're all going after something under the boat. I turn around towards the bow of the boat to see what Mom and Dad are doing. They're not there.

"Mom. Dad." I spin around and yell into the cabin below. I run below thinking they wouldn't leave me in the water to take a nap but do so anyway. I trip in the main cabin and fall face first into the cold water. I get up and run into their cabin. It's empty. "No," I yell. "Mom! Dad!

I run back through the main cabin and up the stairs to go back outside, I trip on the last step hitting my face against the starboard winch. I run to the front of the boat feeling blood dripping down my cheek.

They're not here. I feel the thumps of the sharks hitting the bottom of the boat, I look over the side. A torso attached to a wire. No legs, arms or head. Just a torso and the sharks are fighting over it.

"No," I scream. "Leave him alone! Go away!"

I run to the cabin and grab the riffle and ammunition from the closet. I'm sobbing as I load the gun. It takes over a minute with my hands shaking so badly. I run back outside. The sharks are fighting over the last piece of torso. I fire six shots, starting with the largest shark.

"Fuck you. Fuck you. Fuck you," I cry.

I empty the gun. Blood from the bullet wounds floats to the surface. Suddenly a group of the sharks attacks the shark I shot first. I collapse sobbing on the deck. If I hadn't been tossed from school, Mom and Dad would have left two weeks earlier and avoided this storm. This is my fault. I smash my head against the deck floor until I can't do it anymore. I see black. I'm out.

18

Mercedes

I left the art department at 1 am and thought I saw some-one's shadow disappear down the hall. But I knew, I was tired and it was nothing. No students are allowed out of their rooms after 10 pm, so the campus was empty as I walked to my dorm, but it didn't feel like I was alone.

Hanging from my door to greet me was a dead rat. She was black with a white belly. She was one of the lab rats in biology class that the students had just gotten pregnant with artificial insemination. Now she was dead and hanging by her neck. Her eyes open. She was so innocent – so beautiful. "I'm sorry little one," I said and loosened the noose from her neck and took her from the door. Her body was still soft. I kissed her forehead and walked her outside. I wanted to give her a proper burial. A few bikes were locked to a rack next to the dorm. I turned the quick release from the frame of one of the bikes and removed the seat post, leaving the bike without a seat, and walked into the woods. I found a spot twenty feet from a brook where the remains of an old stone foundation lay, dug a hole with the seat post, and laid her down.

"You're free to roam," I said and covered her with dirt. "Free to love. Free to be. Fly with the angels."

19

Nathan

It's cold. I open my eyes. Bright lights. Stars. They're everywhere, bursting with life, competing to see who can shine the brightest. A shooting star streaks across the sky. Then another. How could the sky be so beautiful at a time like this? For the second time in my life, a rage builds inside me. How dare there be beauty when my mom and dad are dead. I scream as loud as I can. I scream until I can't scream anymore.

I head back down into the cabin, I realize I'm crying. How is it possible to cry so much? I walk into Mom and Dad's cabin and crawl under their down comforter. I want to be close to them. Their smell is on the comforter cover that I pull over my head. I hug one of their pillows and in a fetal position I cry myself to sleep.

I'm happy to be out of the nightmare when I wake up. My parent's bed? For a split second, reality is lost, and life is normal – until I see the water in the cabin. I scream at the top of my lungs. I scream until my throat is raw. I go back to sleep.

My tongue is swollen and stuck to the roof of my mouth. The

sun is beating down on the boat, the cabin feels like a sauna. I get up and grab a bottle of water from one of the storage bins. I know the water is going down my throat, because I see the bottle empting out, but I don't feel it on my throat that's raw from screaming. I'm physically and mentally drained. My soul is empty. I feel nothing as I walk around the inside of the boat and take inventory. One port window is cracked, one is missing. Water in the hull is still ankle deep. I turn the radio on - it doesn't work.

Outside things are worse. The front mast is missing. The main mast is bent in half and leaning forward. Two of the lines that helped hold the mast in place yesterday, are now dangling from it, the bolts at the end of the lines that were attached to the deck are swinging in the air. The jet ski is gone - the rowboat is gone – the extra fuel is gone. The line that was attached to my dad is in the water.

The sky is clear, and in the far distance I see the horizon. I don't know how many nautical miles, but I'm confident it's California - maybe Canada, and the breeze seems to be blowing us towards it. The storm must have pushed us back to where we were five days ago.

I pull the safety line out of the water and coil it up. Mom must have tried to save him. Of course she did. They loved me a lot - but they loved each other more. Mom knew she had no chance of saving him or surviving, but she left her seat to go after him - she had to. Were they able to make eye contact? Were they able to hold onto each other? What were their last thoughts? I go back to their room and cry myself to sleep again.

20

I wake up knowing exactly what I need to do. I'm energized and focused. I get out from under the comforter, walk outside and dive off the stern of the boat, and do breast stroke straight down towards the bottom of the ocean.

The deeper I swim, the better I feel. I increase my speed. The water gets colder and motivates me to swim faster. My lungs start to push against my chest. I feel a connection to the ocean. I feel peace even though my lungs feel like they're going to explode. My vision starts to blur. I will my body to swim deeper and then I try to do somersaults under the water so I won't be able to figure out which way is up if I change my mind. At the start of the second somersault, I see yellow spots, purple spots. Yep, I'm done. I'm drowning. I'm calm. I start leaving my body. I'm on my way, Mom. Sorry Dad.

I'm floating. My head is out of the water. *How did I get here?* I'm in a bear hug, my stomach compresses and I puke. I'm holding onto a handle in the stern of the boat. I puke again. Salt water comes out my nose and mouth. I'm scared. I can't

75

breathe because I'm puking so much. My head goes back under the water, but this time I'm not calm, I'm full of panic. I want to live. I reach for a rope that's hanging off the stern and pull myself up enough so I can lock my right elbow around the first step of the built-in ladder and I puke again. I start to dry heave and feel like I'm going pass out. With every bit of energy I have left I climb the four steps up the boat and collapse on the back deck and pass out.

21

Seagulls singing wake me up. I open my eyes and directly in front of me, standing on the stern of the boat, is one of them staring down at me. I move my eyes to the music another one is making from above the boat as it glides down towards the stern with its wings spread wide, then, after flapping its wings twice, it lands and sits next to the other seagull. Both seem to be looking at me. The sun has started to set. There's a steady breeze, the sky behind the seagulls is full of color – reds, oranges and yellows. It's beautiful. The seagulls chirp loudly, raising and lowering their heads, and then they turn away from me and fly off, looking back once as if to say, "Come on, enough is enough. Let's go."

I can see land. I'm guessing it's five miles away. I grab the binoculars and see a small cove. That will be my goal. Goals are good. I go below deck and grab the main sail from the front storage and jury-rig it onto the bent mast, raising it only a quarter of the way up. If I go any higher the pressure from the wind will rip the mast down. The wind is behind me so I lock

77

the tiller in place so the boat will steer it self, and go down to the cabin and make three peanut butter and jelly sandwiches. I eat them quickly and drink two bottles of water. Immediately my energy level increases.

I grab the hand sump pump and pump all the water out of the hull. It takes over an hour but the boat is lighter and moves faster. I grab a cushion out of storage to sit on and then unlock the tiller and steer the boat towards the mountains. If the wind holds up, I might be able to set anchor before it gets dark.

It feels good to be moving – to have a purpose.

I make it to the cove as the sun disappears behind the horizon. There's not a lot of protection, but I'm not worried and I drop the anchor anyway. This boat is already damaged and if I get blown onto shore – no big deal, a few rocks on a sandy beach. I hear cars and the occasional motorcycle flying around corners high above and hidden behind trees and brush. The beach is narrow and joins a steep mountain with no path down or up, which makes this my own private beach. Exactly what I didn't want. The climb up will be a bitch. And there is no way of sailing out of here with the way the wind is blowing.

I clean up the boat and go through everything to figure out what I'll take with me and what I'll leave behind. The dingy and jet ski were lost in the storm, but I still have a survival raft that I could open up and row to shore. I decide to try and start the boat first to see if I can find a harbor or better place to get off. Dad taught me the basics of engine troubleshooting. I check the spark plugs for water, follow all the wires I can find and then try to get a spark. After an hour, I give up and go back to packing so I can get an early start tomorrow morning. Two pairs of pants, two pairs of shorts, two T-shirts, one long-sleeve shirt, four sets of underwear and the thin leather jacket Mom gave me before we left on the trip, that to my dad's horror she had had custom made in Italy. It fits me perfectly and I love how it feels, and how it is new but looks old. Dad wasn't into spending thousands of dollars on clothing. Mom and I weren't either. But she said she wanted me to have something I would cherish a long time, and a jacket could last a hundred years if taken care of. "You can give it to your kids," she told me.

I open the safe and take all the cash. Dad had said we left with five hundred thousand dollars so I'm guessing that's what's here. He said the cash was for emergencies only. We paid for fuel, food and everything else with credit cards. You would think that much money would take a large suitcase, but it fits easily in the bottom compartment of my backpack. I put my clothes and my iPad in the top compartment. I fill the side pockets with water, snacks, my ATM card, an American Express card, and a Visa for the spots that don't take Amex. Money's never been a worry for me. As Mom and Dad would say, *You're spoiled without being spoiled.*

I bring my pack into my parents' cabin and, as I'm putting it down, I see a USB drive floating in the little water that remains in the far corner of their cabin. Dad had been loading USB drives with information the Russians had on the Americans. I'd forgotten all about that. He was clearly upset when I walked in on him. I look around for others, but don't see any. I put the USB drive in a small slot hidden in the lower right side pocket of my pack, behind the snacks.

I still don't have cell reception and, with our satellite system broken, all forms of communication are lost. I decide there is no sense in going up that hill in the dark. I'll get a good night's sleep and head out in the morning – then I'll hitch a ride to the closest town and call Paul White, my dad's life-long lawyer, mentor and friend.

22

I wake up before sunrise. The cove is quiet. There's a mist floating a foot above the water. A school of small fish jumps in the air and back into the water, making ripples that I watch disappear. I have two bowls of shredded wheat cereal and a bag of almonds.

I grab the emergency safety raft and pull hard on the inflate line – it explodes into shape. I tie the raft to the stern of the boat, and go below to brush my teeth and shave the peach fuzz from my face. I'm ready to go – but having trouble leaving. I walk back into Mom and Dad's cabin. The smell brings Mom back to me – she's hugging me. I pull my Swiss army knife out of my front pocket, unfold the pair of scissors, and cut a 12" by 12" piece of material from the comforter cover, hold it to my face while I breathe in, and then fold it and put it into in my pocket. I'm ready.

The road above is quiet. I guess 5:30 in the morning isn't a popular time in northern California. I take one last look around the boat and grab my backpack and start to load it into the raft when I hear the thundering sound of a motorcycle screaming in the distance. I put the pack down and look up at the mountains just as a motorcycle and rider come flying into view between the trees and then into the air above me. *My god*. I watch as it crash-lands half way down the steep slope between two rocks. For a split second, the rider and bike come to a complete stop from the force of the impact. Then, like from a slingshot, they are tossed into the air again and the rider is thrown off the bike. The rider goes left and the bike goes right. I watch as the bike hits a large cactus, ripping it in two and then ricochets off a rock and smashes onto the beach. Somehow, the rider stops rolling about fifty feet from the beach.

I grab the binoculars from the cabin and zoom in on him. He's wearing a thick black leather jacket with a Hell's Angels logo on it. His forehead is cut open. His index finger twitches. He's alive. I grab the first-aid kit, hop in the life raft and start paddling as fast as I can to shore. The life raft is round and made to keep you alive in rough seas. It's not made for transportation, so every time I paddle the raft wants to spin in a circle. After a few false starts, I begin to figure it out and make my way to shore.

I start to run up the hill. It's really steep and a bitch to climb. For every two forward steps I take, I slip back at least one. *Isn't there a song, Two steps forward and one step back?*

23

The guy is huge. Rough looking. My guess is 6'4", 230 lbs. His chest is moving. He's lost some blood but not enough to be critical. The cut on his forehead is to the bone and runs four inches across.

"Hey, can you hear me?" I ask. He reeks of booze. "I'm going to stitch you up." One of the many home schooling classes Mom and Dad had set up for me was survival skills. We always carried a medical kit with us and we all knew how to do basic sutures, which is a lot easier than it sounds. I have smelling salts, but I don't dare to use them yet – I'd rather this guy be out. I thread the needle and stitch him up as quickly as I can. Satisfied with my work, I put the needle into a hazard bag of cleaner and put it back in the kit. I move my hands all around his chest, his arms and each of his legs checking for broken bones, I don't feel any. I break open one of the smelling salts and put it under his nose. His eyes flutter open. His pupils are small. Scary small. I'm frozen and look into his eyes, not knowing what to do next. He grabs me by the neck with both hands. I didn't even see him move. He's squeezing hard.

"Who the fuck are you?" he asks in a loud, raspy voice.

I can't breathe, but out of muscle memory I throw both my arms up from underneath his and then bring them back down as fast and hard as I can, smashing my elbows into both of his arms. It's a basic Taekwondo move that always works in training. This time, however, it works on only his left arm, leaving his right hand still wrapped around my neck. Somehow, his grip gets stronger. He's looking right at me, his eyes full of hate, he's trying to kill me. *I have to do something now.* I lift my left hand quickly as if to hit him - he looks at it, and with my right hand I thrust my index and middle fingers into his right eyeball. It's a move that's taught but not practiced in most of the advanced martial arts classes. He lets go of my neck and reaches for his eye. I roll off him and scramble down the hill, falling and sliding to the bottom. I run to the life raft, push it off shore and jump in and start rowing. It goes into a circle again, but I'm able to straighten it out faster than before and reach the boat. I tie the raft to the stern with a quick clover hitch and pull myself on board.

He either came after me, or fell down the rest of the hill, because now he's on his hands and knees on the beach, mumbling to himself. I go into the cabin and get the pistol from the safe and go back outside. He's standing when I come back out on deck, and looking up towards the mountain where he came down. He stumbles forward, but catches his balance. He turns around, looks at me on the boat.

"You're lucky you survived," I yell.

"Survive?" He yells. "I wasn't trying to survive, asshole."

Okay. I look up again at where he came down the mountain. There is only one area with sand exposed on the entire mountainside, probably from a past mudslide. He landed on the only spot that wouldn't kill him. I start to laugh at the absurdity of how lucky or unlucky he was.

"What the fuck is so funny?"

I can't stop laughing. The insanity of everything that has happened the past few days – and now this.

"If you were trying to kill yourself you did a pretty lousy job," I say laughing. "Look at where you went off, where you landed the first time, where you landed the second time. Someone out there must be looking out for you."

He turns away from me and looks up the mountain. His shoulders start to raise and lower, then he screams. A long Tarzan-like scream, and falls to his knees. "God damn it!" he yells into the sky.

"Look, if you don't want any help, that's fine. I just lost my mom and dad in this storm – they're gone. Stitching you up, helping you, that gave me a little boost. But if you want to kill yourself - go ahead. Why don't you fill your pockets with rocks and then walk into the ocean. Now, that's commitment. Hell, anyone can ride a motorcycle off the side of a mountain," I yell.

"I could empty my pockets. I could turn around. I did commit. I rode off a fucking cliff," he says.

He's got a point

"Okay, but if you walk into the water with your pockets full of rocks – you really got to want to end it, because whatever you think is so bad now, probably won't seem so when you're struggling for oxygen. I bet the second you rode off the cliff you knew you made a mistake. You didn't want to die," I say.

He drops to his knees again and sobs.

Welcome to my world.

He stops crying, pulls a pack of cigarettes out of his jacket pocket, lights one and sits on the beach. He still looks angry. I put the pistol in the back of my shorts and climb into the raft, and as slowly as I can, I paddle towards shore. This time the raft moves forward without going into circles getting me to shore faster. *Great.* I hear the raft scrape the bottom of the ocean stopping me a foot from shore. I need to see what he does before I get out of the raft. I move the pistol from the back of my shorts and put it between my legs.

Maybe this isn't such a good idea. I push the raft back off the bottom and away from the beach.

He starts turning around slowly. I rest my right hand on the handle of the pistol. He's facing me. The rage that filled his face is gone. His facial muscles look relaxed. He almost looks nice.

"I've lost everything," he says. "My wife. My kids. My house. I have nothing left to live for."

The raft drifts a few feet further from shore.

"Lost – meaning they're dead?" I ask.

"My son is doing a life sentence. My daughter, she hasn't spoken to me in two years. My wife left me, I don't even remember when."

"Are you hungry?" I ask him, using a lesson Dad taught me on how to break people's self pity by asking a question that has nothing to do with the topic they're on.

"Am I what?" he asks.

"Are you hungry?"

He shakes his head side to side and almost smiles. "Who the hell knows?"

"Well, let's make some sandwiches and find out," I say.

His weight lowers the raft a lot. He looks at the gun between my legs. It's within his reach.

I hand him the paddle and to my surprise he paddles the raft to the boat without spinning us around. "Do you know how to use it"? He asks as the raft hits the stern of the sailboat.

"What?"

He looks at the pistol. I shake my head yes.

He gets out first. I move the pistol to the back of my shorts and climb out after him. We each eat a peanut butter and jelly sandwich, an apple and some almonds. I tell him about the storm but don't go into much detail, telling him I've already processed it and need to move on. "How old are you, kid?" he asks me.

"Eighteen," I say.

"Shit, you look a lot younger. You're a smart kid."

"What's your name?" I ask.

"Rusty. Russell but I go by Rusty."

"Yours?"

"Nathan. So check it out, Rusty. We get to climb back up that hill," I say.

"I'm not walking up that damn thing and giving the mountain the satisfaction of taunting me the entire way back up. I'll check out the motor," he says.

Two hours later Rusty gets the boat running and we're headed north. For the next couple of hours Rusty goes over the joys of riding a Harley Davidson and how it's an entirely different ride from any other motorcycle. Beads of sweat fill the pores on his face and start dripping off onto the deck. I try not to stare, but somehow he notices. "It's the booze," he says, and wipes his forehead.

"Careful with those stitches," I say.

He asks how I learned to stitch someone up and I tell him about some of my home schooling experiences.

24

By two o'clock we are docked in Carmel Harbor. I lock the pistol in the safe, grab my cell charger and plug it into an outlet attached to the dock. I call my dad's attorney, tell him what happened, then I call the police department. Twenty minutes later I'm sitting with two local cops in the cabin of the boat filling out a report and answering questions.

"This pistol has been used recently. By who?" One of the cops asks. They had asked me if any weapons were on board so I gave them the pistol from the safe.

"Me" I say. "I shot at the sharks."

"You used the gun to shoot sharks?" He looks at me, then at his partner. I didn't like him.

"Yes. They were feeding on what was left of my dad's body."

They look at each other again. "Where are the emergency supplies?" They ask.

I brought them out and handed the box to the closest cop.

"No flare gun?" He asks.

"No, my mom must have used it when I was out."

They look over the boat again, this time taking pictures.

"Don't understand why your mom would go outside," the shorter cop says.

"You wouldn't go outside for your wife?" I ask him.

"Hell no," he says.

"But you'd go out for Amy," the other cop says. They give each other a look.

I pop my head out of the cabin and look up at the harbor restaurant's outside deck. Rusty stands out from the crowd that's dressed in bright colored Polo shirts and shorts as he drinks beer from a large mug. He had told me a drink was the only way to stop the sweating, and he was going to quit drinking but he couldn't do it cold turkey cause it would kill him.

My pack is sitting right next to him holding all the cash. I'm not worried about it. I have the American Express, Visa and the ATM in my wallet. I think about what Mom and Dad pounded into my head. Money was to be used for your freedom, your mental and physical health, it's for adventure, and for helping others. If Rusty steals my pack with the money – so be it. Dad's lawyers told me to remove the cash from the boat before the cops arrived in case they were crooked.

"Okay kid. Sign here," the taller cop says.

I sign the paper and the cops walk away from the boat. I follow them with my eyes and watch as they look at Rusty on the deck. A waitress brings him another large mug of beer. Dad made me watch videos on alcoholism and drug addiction once a month for ten years. These were not feel-good videos. They were filled with hardcore real life people going through detox. Some strapped down to tables, some to chairs, most covered in their own vomit, some puking a lot of blood. Bankers, lawyers, doctors, street people – it didn't matter. They all looked the same while they detoxed. Dad always said: "Alcoholism doesn't care who it gets, just as long as it gets someone. Booze is like oxygen for an alcoholic." He said it was in our genes and we couldn't risk using it. I never saw my dad with a drink.

25

I am still thinking about my dad's conversation as I walk up to Rusty on the deck.

"How did it go?" He asks.

"I'll make a deal with you." I say, reaching for his mug of beer. He pulls it towards himself. His eyes narrow. His facial muscles tighten.

"You're too young," he says.

"This isn't for me. I have an idea. Just hear me out and then you can drink your beer. Please. Put it down."

"He puts the beer down. "You got two minutes kid." He no longer looks nice.

"Promise me, you'll listen to what I have to say without drinking till I'm done," I say.

He just stares at me.

"Promise me."

"Okay," he says.

"Is that a promise?"

"Jesus, kid. Yes, it's a promise. Now you got a minute."

"Thank you. Okay, I want you to remember the last time you hugged your daughter. I want you to remember how it felt. Think about her smile, the last time you saw her laugh. Now, I want you to think about your daughter two years from now laughing with you. The two of you are together hugging and laughing. Think about holding her child, your grandchild. Think about what kind of grandfather you are going to be. Now, I want you to think about your son," Rusty's facial muscles tighten up. "Think about the man you want to become so that you can show your son that anything is possible in life if you set your mind to it and work towards it. Rusty, I want you to really picture the man you want to become. Take your time." And I do give him time to think about it.

"Are you a sober man or a drunk man?"

Rusty opens his eyes and looks at me. He shakes his head. "Sober."

"Now, I want you to think about what you want to do for a living. What is it that you'd love to do?" I ask.

"Own a motorcycle repair shop that specializes in Harley Davidsons and sells bikes too."

"Okay, Now I want you to visualize that successful shop of yours. See yourself opening the doors in the morning. Turning on the lights to start the day. See the bikes lined up in the showroom, see the bikes in the garage waiting to be repaired. Now, look down at the beer on the table. Look at that mug of poison that is the only thing that can separate you from your dreams."

I let him think it over.

"Now, take a sip of that poison, and tell me, no, ask yourself, is continuing to drink that poison worth giving up the man you want to become? The man you know you can become?" I ask, feeling as if Dad's wisdom is flowing through me.

I know I've gotten through. Rusty stares down at the mug of beer. He picks it up slowly, puts it to his lips and puts it back down on the table.

"Whenever you're ready," the waitress says, putting our bill on the table.

Rusty pulls a twenty and a five-dollar bill from his wallet and puts them on the table. "Thanks. It's all set," he says.

"I don't care how you quit drinking, Rusty, but you owe it to yourself, and to your family."

"Why do you know so much about addiction?"

"My dad exposed me to the dangers of booze. He never drank or did drugs. I haven't either. But from what he told me, alcoholism runs in our family."

Rusty looks like he wants to say something but doesn't.

"If you get me to the East Coast – I'll help you open that bike shop," I say.

Rusty looks at me and laughs.

"I'm serious. I'm rich, Rusty. Let's go buy us a Harley and ride to the East Coast."

"Are you fucking serious?"

"If Harleys are as good as you say, it will be more fun than driving a car, and I'm too young to rent a car."

"You are one interesting kid," he says.

I send for an Uber and then try calling Mercedes. Her voice-mail doesn't come on. I'm not ready to FaceTime her. Seeing her would be too much. I send her a text saying I love her and will call her again.

26

Two hours later Rusty and I are wearing skull caps and going 75 mph. I'm sitting in a sidecar that is attached to a used 2006 Harley Davidson Road King. It had 4,558 miles on it. The dealer was asking $29,999. We settled for $24,000 in cash. "Helmets that are legal but don't do shit," Rusty had said about the skull caps.

"Where the hell did you get that kind of cash and why the hell aren't you eating?" Rusty had asked me at McDonalds while we waited for them to clean up the bike and put a new battery in it. I wasn't about to open my pack in front of Rusty or the salesman, so I went to the bathroom ahead of time, knowing we were going to buy a bike, and put thirty-five thousand in the top of my pack, pretending it was all I had.

"It was in our safe for emergencies. This is kind of an emergency. That leaves us with eleven thousand to ride east."

"Jesus, kid. We could ride across the country three times on eleven grand."

Rusty takes a bite of his Big Mac. "You're a unique kid."

I take one of his fries.

They are good. Really good.

"Buy your own damn fries," he says, laughing. "No wonder your so goddamn skinny, you don't eat."

"One of my parents' cardinal rules was no fast food. Ever. No exceptions," I tell him.

I wasn't about to break that rule. But damn, that was a really good fry. I take one more and realize I've already broken the rule, so I go to the counter and order a Big Mac, French fries and a Vanilla milk shake. I love every bite of it. Sorry Mom – sorry Dad.

27

We're headed to Rusty's house in Stockton, CA so he can pay his rent and tie up some loose ends before we head east tomorrow morning.

My iPhone is plugged in and I'm listening to the Record Company on my headphones that fit easily over the skullcap. It's the first time I've been at peace since the storm.

It feels like I'm flying as we blow past cars on the 5 freeway chilling to good music.

I send Mercedes another text, then open Safari on my cell phone and type in one of the URL's that Dad made me memorize in the car. A page shows up with two small boxes, one for a name, one for a password. I type in my information and wait as a second page fills the screen with over twenty links. I click on the first one. Dad's face appears, he's smiling and looking right at me. I click play. "Hey. So we didn't make it. Remember the lessons, Nathan. You go for it in life. This trip that your mom and I went on was an adventure. Life's an adventure. You have got to do things with your life, Son. Positive things, things you believe in, things that move you and that inspire you. You don't have to go and climb Mount Everest. Adventures are so much more than the physical extremes. Adventures are a way of life. Teaching kids can be an adventure, as can be starting a business; learning and organic farming can also be adventures. It's all about the path you take and your frame of mind. Remember, especially now, in order to be happy – you have to spread happiness and inspire others, while you search for others who inspire you. I'm still with you, Son. Keep up with your meditation practice, I know you will. Exercise, eat a healthy diet, and learn something every day – keep those things in check and you'll be fine. Mind, body and spirit. Go get 'em, Son. Have fun, be fun, spread fun. Talk to you soon." I close Safari, lean back in the sidecar, and use my sweatshirt as a pillow. Sleep comes quickly.

28

Stockton, CA

A drop in the air temperature wakes me up just as the sun is setting. The street is lined with houses with foreclosure signs on the front lawns. The sidewalks are empty. A black Honda Civic pulls alongside us. It's low to the ground, has racing wheels, tinted windows and the engine is loud enough that you can hear it over the Harley. The driver's window goes down. A tough-looking Mexican guy wearing a cap sideways stares at us and takes a large hit off a vape pipe. He smiles. "Nice ride," he says and takes off ahead of us.

A few blocks later we pull into a narrow driveway and stop in front of a small white stucco house. The windows and front door have metal gates over them. Rusty gets off the bike and punches a five-digit code into the security system. The garage door opens up and we pull in. The house is small but much cleaner than I thought it would be. The furniture is old, but really cool looking. A large brown leather couch, a retro red leather chair, and a wooden bookshelf that looks like it's from the 1800s. Two vintage framed posters of Harley Davidsons are on one wall, and an oil painting of I don't know what is on the other living room wall. Whatever the painting is, I like it and can't stop looking at it. Rusty opens a couple of windows. "I'm going out to settle up with the landlord. You get the couch. The bathroom is down on the right. Sheets and blanket are in the closet."

"Do you have Wi-Fi?" I ask.

"Yeah, the password is Harley5."

"Good one," I say laughing. "A fifth grader with a cell phone could hack you in ten minutes."

"You're paranoid, kid. I got nothing to hide."

"You got bars on your windows and front door. You might as well take them off and leave the front door wide open. Your identity is worth three grand on the dark web," I tell him.

"Change it for me," Rusty says and takes off.

I try FaceTiming Mercedes.

"Nathan," she says, answering right away.

"I was getting worried about you," I tell her.

"Worried about me? Oh, my god, Nathan, I'm so glad you guys are all right."

"We uh... We uh... They didn't make it." I start crying. Hearing Mercedes' voice, her warmth, the love coming from her voice makes me lose control of my emotions. Memories of Mom laughing with her at the picnic table come to mind. The way Mom went on and on about how beautiful Mercedes' artwork was the whole drive home from school. I break down crying and put my face on my arms to cover the tears. Finally, my crying has worked its way out. I look up from my arms and into Mercedes' eyes. She's still crying. We look into each other's eyes, not saying a word. I want nothing else more in life then to be able to climb into her arms and melt. "They prepared me for years on how to live without out them. I thought I was dealing with it okay – I guess I'm not. I'm sorry," I say.

"It's okay to cry Nathan – you should be crying. I love you," she whispers.

"I love you," I say.

The door behind Mercedes flies open. A heavy-set woman in underwear and a bra walks past the frame. "You got any clean shirts?" she asks.

"Please, get out of my room. I'm on the phone," Mercedes snaps at the woman.

"Don't give me no back-talk. If you didn't get that boy in trouble you'd be in your dorm room instead of home."

"Take whatever you want and get out," Mercedes yells.

With a cigarette hanging from her mouth, the woman walks out carrying a bunch of shirts.

"My stepmom. Now you've met them both via the Internet," Mercedes says.

"Get your GED."

"My what?" she asks.

"Your GED, that way you can still go to college if you want."

"I'll do anything to get out of here."

As if on cue, yelling comes from behind her door.

"The god damn car is out of gas," her stepmother yells.

"I should go," Mercedes says.

"Wake the fuck up Harry," her stepmother yells.

"I'm coming to get you, two weeks tops, maybe one. Find out about that test. We'll both take it."

"I love you," She says.

"God damn gas in the car bitch," screams a man.

""Bye," she says.

"Bye," I say and the screen goes black.

29

For a guy with such a rough exterior, Rusty's house was surprisingly spotless. Sitting on a small bookshelf in the living room was a photo of him with what must be his two kids. In the picture, Rusty is lean and muscular, with long hair. He looks more like a rock star hanging at home between gigs then a biker in a gang.

In the bathroom, there are two photos side by side, the first one is a group of twelve guys in fatigues; some are holding knives, some pistols, and a few with machine guns hanging over their shoulders. They're in a desert somewhere, and all have cigarettes hanging from their mouths; and there is no mistaking Rusty, he's one of three that are each leaning back against a black Ninja motorcycle. His stare gives me the chills. The other photo has eight men, each one leaning against a Harley Davidson smoking cigarettes on a coastal road with the ocean in the background. It's the same group of guys - less four. In the first photo they're all ripped and look like wide receivers on an NFL football team; in the second they're all out of shape, especially Rusty.

"Three died over there in Iraq. One here of an overdose," Rusty says walking past the open door holding a pizza box.

"I didn't hear you come in," I say, wanting to ask him about his experience in Iraq.

"So what's your plan for our trip east?" Rusty asks.

"We ride to NYC first, so I can meet with my dad's lawyer to take care of some stuff he has for me. While I'm there, I'll have him write up a contract for your bike business. Then we can ride to my house in Bedford, NY and pick up the van. I'll drive the van to Mercedes' house in North Carolina, and you can ride the Harley back and get the business started."

"You're serious?"

"Yeah, we made a deal - I'll front the money, you run the business. Twenty-five, seventy-five. I get twenty-five percent of all profits, you get seventy-five percent." I say.

"You can really get the money?"

"I can really get the money. Dad taught me to invest in people with passion, pride and persistence. He called it his triple-play rule. I know you have the passion and the pride – just not sure about the persistence. But I gave you my word," I say, looking at him and then back to the more recent photo. "After this pizza though, no more junk food. You're going to get back into shape - like this guy," I say pointing at him in the first photo. "Fighting shape to protect my investment. Green juices, fruits, vegetables, nuts, fish."

"For a kid that looks fifteen, you sure as shit sound wise," he says, "or stupid," he laughs.

30

We take off the next morning at 6 am and ride all day and night, stopping only for gas and to use the bathroom. On our second stop, Rusty takes off his helmet and jacket. His shirt is soaked in sweat and his hair looks like he just walked out of the shower. "It's the booze kid," he says looking in pain. "Thankfully, I had bought a bunch of snacks at Whole Foods as we rode out of California, because I knew that once we got on the main highway headed east, everything was going to be fast food. Fresh cut vegetables, almond butter, Stonehouse blueberry jam and a loaf of bread. "Sixty bucks for that bag? No cigarettes, no chew, no coke, no Bud, how the hell does this place stay in business?" he asked the cashier.

Every time I hand him something to eat, he just shakes his head no. Instead, at every stop he buys two large black coffees that he drinks while eating bread with nothing on it. "It helps absorb the acid," he tells me.

"You've got to start eating some of the vegetables," I say. And to his credit he finally does - one carrot and a stick of celery.

"It's a start, kid," he says, looking worn out from the ride.

I'm worried about Mercedes' living situation and want to see her as soon as possible, so I push Rusty to keep riding. But at 11 pm he has had enough. We pull over at a Courtyard Marriott; one of the hotels my dad's company has a corporate account with, and we get a room. On the way to the elevator, we walk past the bar. Rusty looks at it like a dog looks at a bone.

"You okay?" I ask.

"I need to shower," he grunts.

And Rusty does, he takes a shower right away and I order room service. White fish, chicken, asparagus, green beans and salad.

We share stories as we eat. After my endless probing, Rusty starts opening up. He talks a little about some of his childhood. He's one of three kids. "Mom was a nursery school teacher, Dad a part-time construction worker and full-time drunk. They were good people though. Lost them a few years back."

Growing up he loved football and had been the starting quarterback for his junior high. But his passion for girls, booze and pot won out. Joining the military was his mom's idea. She thought it would straighten him out. And it did, for a bit. He worked his way up to Delta Force, an elite group of men, similar to the Navy Seals. When I ask him why he left, all he says is, "My time was up."

I tell him more about Mom and Dad and my home schooling. We watch some television, switching between Stephen Colbert and Jimmy Fallon.

For the next three days we ride, stopping only for gas and to get a hotel. We are making good time, riding over seven

110

hundred miles a day. If traffic isn't bad, we'll be in New York City tomorrow, late afternoon.

We check into another Marriott, this one in Cleveland, Ohio, and eat a late dinner at the restaurant attached to the lobby.

"Let's stop in Troy, NY tomorrow. One of my military buddies that I haven't seen since Iraq lives there. If we spend the night there we can get an early start for the city and you can get all your stuff done in one day, " he says.

Rusty is burned out, and it would be cool to meet one of his army buddies. "Why not," I say.

31

We roll into Troy, a town that has a similar feel to Stockton, CA, but without the palm trees. Both towns have a hard edge to them. We ride down Main Street, passing tattoo parlors, fast food restaurants and liquor stores. Rusty pulls the bike into a Red Roof Inn parking lot that sits right next to a run-down looking bar. Harleys, beat up pick-ups and old vans fill the lot. I get a sick feeling in my gut. *This is not a good idea.*

Rusty's mood has changed in the past six hours. On our last stop for gas, he barely said a word to me. He was fidgety and in a hurry to get back on the bike.

Rusty snaps at the hotel clerk when she asks for his driver's license so she can make a copy of it.

"What you mean, you want to make a copy of it?"

"Fa Secureeetee," the woman says in broken English.

"What's up with the attitude?" I ask him.

"Spent, kid."

We walk up two flights of old concrete stairs to room 218. The window looks out front so we can keep an eye on the bike. Rusty goes into the bathroom. I have to exercise. I have to do something – anything to calm my mind that is spinning a million miles an hour. I start doing a set of fifty push-ups, then a second set. I finish up the third set and I hear Rusty having a muffled conversation on his cell phone. But I can't make out what he's saying. I jump up to start my squats. Rusty walks out of the bathroom.

"I'm headed next door to meet my buddy. You're on your own for dinner."

"You're meeting him at a bar?" I ask.

"Yeah, a bar. They serve food. You got a problem with that?"

"Whatever," I say.

He walks out, leaving the door to shut itself. I feel as if something else has shut too. I've never seen anyone's personality change so quickly. I look around the room that suddenly feels like a prison cell. The beds are only three feet apart. The blankets have cigarette burns on them. The carpet is lined with stains and more burns.

I try FaceTiming Mercedes while looking at my pack across the room with half a million dollars in it. I'm antsy from sitting all day. I need to run - I have to run. My head feels like it's going to explode. On the sixth ring - I hang up, put my shorts and running shoes on, grab a credit card and a fifty dollar bill and put them in my sock and then head out.

32

I immediately feel better, my legs go into autopilot, my stride lengthens, my pace quickens, my mind slows down. Yes, running is my Adderall. I have no idea how far I've run. I'm guessing six, seven or eight miles, because I feel my body feeding my runner's high. It's dark – when did it get dark?

A loud beep comes on from behind me. A cop car pulls up alongside of me, slowing down to match my speed. The window goes down. The lights on the roof start spinning in blue.

"Where you headed?" the cop asks.

"Not sure," I say.

"Not a good answer. What are you running from?"

"Not running from anything," I say laughing. "Actually, that's not true. I'm running to clear my head. Don't you run?" I ask.

"Where you staying?"

"What makes you think I don't live here?" I ask.

"That's obvious."

"Red Roof Inn," I say.

The cop eyes me. "Where you from?"

"Bedford, NY."

"What brings you to Troy?"

"The night life," I say. He doesn't smile. "Just passing though on the way to New York City," I say.

"You got ID?"

"Yea, back at the hotel."

"Stop running, kid."

I stop.

"If I call the hotel, what name should I give them to confirm you're staying there?"

"Nathan Paddington."

He punches a few buttons into his monitor and calls the hotel to confirm I'm staying there.

"So what are you doing in town, Nathan Paddington?"

"Seriously, just passing through," I say.

He stares at me.

"Hey, if you give me a ride to the closest pizza place, I'll buy."

"No can do," he says and drives off, but stops a hundred yards ahead. I run up to his window.

"Subs are faster. Subs are cheaper. I can't let you pay though. Get in the back."

I hop in the back.

"How long have you been a cop for?"

"We like to say police officer," he says and then laughs, "Five years today. I got the job a month after I got back from Iraq."

"Was it really that bad over there? With all this PTSD on the news and stuff, it sounds crazy."

"Wasn't bad for me or most of my buddies. We saw little action except for the occasional road-side bomb. It was mostly fighting boredom, but for guys who were there the first year, yeah, it was bad, real bad. The bummer is a lot of soldiers milk the system, getting benefits they don't need. The vets that have bad PTSD – they refuse treatment.

The restaurant is small, but the food smells good. A handful of other customers and three employees eye us as we walk in, probably wondering what a surfer looking kid was doing eating dinner with a cop in Troy, NY.

We each have a meatball sub and it's as good as it smells. I want to talk to him about Rusty, but decide it's not a good idea. His name is Esteban Estrada. His father was born in Mexico, his mom in the states. I tell him about the sailing trip but not about Luke's Academy or anything about Rusty. Twenty minutes later we head out.

We pull into the parking lot of the Red Roof Inn. Esteban parks the cruiser as the front door of the bar flies open. Rusty has his arm around another biker as they come stumbling out, each holding a bottle of beer. They're noticeably drunk as they light cigarettes and look over at the cruiser.

"America's finest," Esteban says while getting out of the cruiser. Then he walks around to the back door, opening it up to let me out.

"Thanks," I say and shake his hand.

33

I go upstairs and head back into the room and try Mercedes again. She answers on the first ring with her head at an angle so only half her face in on the screen.

"Hey," she answers. "I missed you before."

"Hey."

"I can't wait to see you," she says.

"Me too. We should be there in three days max. Hopefully two."

A tear drops from Mercedes' eye.

"Hey, you're supposed to be happy," I say.

"It's been a crazy couple of days."

"In what way?"

"We can talk about it later," she says.

"What's going on? Why are you hiding your face Mercedes?"

She turns her head. The right side of her face is swollen and red.

"My God," I say.

"My dad. I mean Harry – who, I found out, isn't actually my dad."

"What?"

"We had a blow-out a few nights after I got back from school. He hadn't said a word to me since I got back. He didn't even want me going to Luke's. He said it was a pipe dream and a waste of time. So I asked him, 'What's your deal, Dad? You didn't want me to go to art school and now that I'm back you won't even acknowledge my existence?' I should have waited until morning to talk to him. He was drunk, started going on about my mom, saying I was just like her. Always dreaming. Never willing to settle down. He was yelling at me. Saying Mom was a tramp – she had affairs. 'You're probably not even my daughter,' he screamed. I've never seen him like that, Nathan. He's always had a temper – he always gave me a hard time, but he never hit me. He was pissed off that I wanted to go to Luke's, that's when things started to change between us. Before I decided to go to Luke's, he always made sure I was okay, you know, he'd look out for me in his own weird way. So, it got me thinking, what if my mom really did have an affair? What if he wasn't my dad? I grabbed some hair from his brush and mailed it in along with some of my hair for a DNA test. I also crawled around our attic until I found my mom's journals and read them while I waited the ten days for the test results. She did have an affair on him – and she wrote all about it. She worked at a hotel in town and met a guest named Jean Philip Martin. He was an art professor from France teaching a course at Virginia State for a semester. She was seventeen."

"Hence your art skills," I say.

"Right? So I get the results yesterday. Dad, Harry comes home from work. He's drunk, which has been the norm since I got back, and I tell him he's not my dad. He smacks me across the face and then just stands there staring at me. He didn't say anything. I could see the veins in his face swell. He started to shake. Then his eyes started to well up and he took off."

"Can you spend the night somewhere else?" I ask.

"No, I'll be fine here."

"Where's Jean Philip Martin now?" I ask.

"According to Google, he's an art professor at the University in Paris. He's married with two kids."

"Well - Lets go," I say.

"Yeah, we'll just hop on a plane and fly to Paris," she giggles with tears in her eyes, her face red and swollen unable to hide her beauty.

"Mercedes, we can get the tickets. We'll go meet your dad. I promise."

We talked till two am. I fell asleep on top of the bed fully clothed.

34

I wake up to loud laughing and the sound of the door opening. Rusty and a woman stumble inside. The clock on the bedside table says 4:30 am.

"Take a hike, kid," Rusty says.

"Where do you suggest I go at 4:30?"

"Use your imagination," he says as the woman starts reaching for his belt buckle.

I shake my head and walk out of the room and head down to the lobby, which is the size of a large closet with a TV that's not on and a line of dirty plastic bins that hold various kinds of cereal. I sit on one of the chairs and do my meditation.

An hour later, I head back upstairs to the room. When I open the door, Rusty is passed out in bed snoring, and the woman has the top of my back pack open and is going through it.

"Hey!" I yell.

"You think I fuck for free? That's not the way it works, honey."

I walk up to the pack and look down at the open pocket. She was twenty seconds away from an early retirement – with the half million dollars just one zipper away. I reach into my sock and hand her the fifty-dollar bill I had hidden away for my jog.

"Here, you can have this," I say.

"It's a hundred," she snaps.

"It's fifty or I call the cops."

She takes the fifty and leaves. I lock the door behind her and take a shower. I'm pissed and hoping the hot water will help settle me down, but it doesn't. I have to get back into my daily routine of exercising and meditating. I dry off and put the same clothes back on and open the door to the room. Rusty is sitting up in bed, smoking a cigarette.

35

"**What's your deal?**" I ask.

"My deal?"

"Yes, your deal!" I say slowly and loudly. "Our deal! You not drinking. You getting your life back in order, starting your business, winning your daughter back, getting back into shape?" I yell.

"Mr. fucking wisdom. You don't know shit, kid. You're a rich little shit that doesn't know shit about real life," his words are slurred.

"You rode a motorcycle off a cliff so you could buy back your daughter's love with money. Money. You're a fucking coward, Rusty. Any man that thinks his kids want money more then they want his love is an idiot. You! You're a fucking coward. You're an idiot. You don't have the balls to go see your daughter, you don't have the balls to go see your son in prison!" I'm yelling at him as he gets off the bed and gets in my face.

"Listen, you little trust fund shit. I don't want another word out of you about money, 'cause you grew up with a silver spoon in your mouth. You're a spoiled brat. Fuck you and your daddy's life's lessons."

I glare at him. "My dad never gave me money as a kid. I earned every penny. He gave me opportunity. I spent my summers working the field – waiting tables. I started businesses as a kid. One that I even got franchised – Kids running with Seniors. Could I have done it without him? No. Probably not. Did he buy me things? Yes. Clothes, food, classes, travel, he put a roof over my head. He gave me opportunities – a lot of them. But he never, ever, gave me money for nothing until now. Now that he and my mom are dead. So yes. I have a lot of it and will be getting a lot more of it. But I don't have their love anymore because they're gone. They gave me their unconditional love, twenty-four seven. They always let me know how much they loved me. You? You tried to cash in a life insurance policy and buy your kids' love, because you didn't have the courage to tell them you fucked up their life and yours! You chose booze over your kids' love. You sold your kids out, Rusty! You are a pathetic piece of shit!"

I see Rusty's eyes start to narrow. What I don't see is his left hand until it's too late. Rusty hits me hard on the right side of my face, sending me flying against the wall. The pain is piercing. I stumble forward. My world starts to blur. I fall to my knees. I try to get back up but fall again face first onto the carpet. The smell is rancid. I try doing a push-up to get back to my feet but fall back down. *Breathe Nathan. Breathe. Slow deep breaths.* I do what my mind tells me to, and slowly get up while taking deep breaths. I stagger forward, catch my balance on the corner of the table and, without looking at Rusty, I grab my backpack and head out the door as my eye starts to close up.

"Hey," I hear his voice but can't register what he's saying.

36

I walk as fast as my brain will allow, while it continues to do cartwheels in my skull. One step at a time. Don't look back. In the stairwell, I open the smallest side pocket of my pack and grab the extra key for the Harley and then head outside. I turn around once, to see if Rusty is behind me. He's not. I toss the pack in the sidecar, put on my skull cap, start the bike and take off. As I turn right out of the parking lot I look up towards the hotel room and see Rusty looking out the window. *One of my dad's lessons, Rusty – never show your full hand until you really know the person.* I've had my motorcycle license since I was sixteen. I give him the finger and ride off.

I stop at the first open gas station I see, a Shell, and fill up the bike and go into the bathroom to check out my eye. It looks even worse than it feels and it feels really bad. The cartwheels in my brain have stopped. They have now been replaced by a throbbing headache. I'm pretty sure I have a concussion, so aspirin is out of the question. I have to ride it out. I know, no pun, intended, I'm about to ride out of here on a Harley that's the loudest bike you can buy.

Twenty minutes later I'm on 87 south and focused on my breathing instead of my pain. I have my head turned to the right so the pressure from the wind lands on the left side of my face. How could I have been so wrong about someone? I pull the throttle back, getting the bike up to 75, and put it on cruise control and think about Mercedes. At least we'll both have black eyes. I try to smile.

A roar of thunder snaps me out of my daze. I look in the left side mirrors and see at least a dozen motorcycles racing down the highway – all Harleys. I don't know if I should speed up or slow down, so I maintain my speed as they split off at the last second before hitting me; six bikes go to my right, six go to my left. They have me locked inside a circle of bikes. They're slowing down. I have no choice – I have to match their speed and slow down. They pull over, leading me with them in the breakdown lane. No one speaks. No one moves. A few cars and an eighteen-wheeler pass us; but at this time in the morning the highway is pretty quiet. We sit for five very long minutes. Then I hear another Harley roaring down the highway, it's got to be going over a hundred miles an hour. It comes to a skidding stop behind us. There are two riders on the bike. I look in the side mirror and see Rusty get off the back of the bike and walk towards me. He looks pissed. But I'm done with this. If he wants to shoot me, so be it. But I want to fight him first. If I can get him on the ground I know I can beat him. I trained with the Gracie brothers. He may be a hundred pounds heavier, he may be stronger, but I know what to do.

37

"Hey," Rusty yells.

I turn around – look at him, fluid dripping out of my closed eye.

"Jesus," he says and stops when he sees the damage he did.

"I thought you never rode bitch?" I challenge him.

He smiles – just a little; then his expression turns serious.

"You were right about everything," he starts walking over to me. "Trying to buy my kids' love. I had no right to do that to you – no right. You saved my life kid, I'm sorry for what I said about your dad. He must have been one hell of a good man — 'cause he raised one hell of a good kid."

The sound of police sirens makes us all turn around to look.

"We gotta scram, Rust," one of the bikers yells.

"I'm staying," Rusty says looking at me. "Don't worry, kid. Not going with you."

"You sure?" Another biker asks.

"Never been so sure in my life," says Rusty.

The bikes take off in one thundering roar, leaving Rusty standing next to me on the Harley.

One cop car comes screeching to a stop behind us. Two other cop cars speed past chasing the other bikers.

"Hands above your heads!" a cop yells over the loudspeaker.

"Keep your fingers locked so you don't make any quick moves with your hands," Rusty says, looking at me.

"Words of wisdom?" I ask.

"That's low," Rusty says with a smile.

"Get off the bike," yells one of them. In my side mirror, with only one good eye I see that the cops are now out of the cruiser. One is standing behind the car door with his pistol aimed at Rusty. The other one has his gun aimed at me.

"Now turn around," the one walking up to us says.

Rusty and I turn around and face the cops.

"Nathan? What the hell is going on? What happened to you?" Esteban, the officer I met jogging asks.

"It was an accident," I tell him.

"No accident, officer. I did it. I fucked him up."

"On the ground, now!" Esteban yells.

We start to get on the ground.

"Not you Nathan," Esteban yells.

"You cover the biker, Edoardo, I'll cover the kid," Esteban says to his partner.

"Have to search you Nathan," and he does, checking my pockets, underarms, hair and sneakers. "Okay, turn around and put your hands behind your back. Hopefully, these will be off soon," Esteban says as he handcuffs me.

They run both our licenses. Mine comes up clean. Rusty's doesn't.

"What's going to happen to him?" I ask.

"All depends if he can post bail."

"I'm not going to post bail, kid. I need help. In jail I can get it. Do it right this time. Try to get my life back in order. Maybe get into a state rehab and get sober. Fuck knows I couldn't do it on my own. And you little fucker, not telling me you had your motorcycle license."

"My dad made me learn how to operate cars, bikes, planes and boats in case of an emergency. Got a license for each."

"Come on. We gotta go," the cop says pushing the top of Rusty's head to get him into the back seat.

"Sorry about the eye."

38

I'm an hour away from Mercedes. My stomach is in knots. I start questioning my feelings. Am I really in love with her? Was she really in love with me? My entire body tingles, telling me yes.

I thought about the video of Dad I watched at the restaurant where I had lunch. "Nathan, you're full of love – just like your mom. Use that love and positive energy to make the most out of your life. Explore. Better yourself on a daily basis. Help others better themselves. You have all the resources you need. Take advantage of them. Paul will go over the paperwork with you. He's the only one who knows about what I've set up for you, and you'll need to check in with him three times a year until you're twenty-five. Remember, when you fall down, pick yourself up, dust yourself off and do the next right thing," he said.

39

Three more turns according to my iPhone's GPS. I'm trying not to speed. Trailer parks, prefab houses and seven-elevens line the streets. At every corner there is a Burger King, McDonalds or Wendy's. There's my second right, Bay Shore drive, my heart is pounding, I turn right onto it, and then –oh my god– a quick left into her driveway. It's a white, single story house with a one-foot white picket fence wrapped around it. An old Pontiac Grand Am with missing tires sits on concrete cinder blocks in the driveway. A couple of car batteries are on the front lawn, which looks like it hasn't been cut in months.

The front door flies open – Mercedes runs out with her arms open and a huge smile on her face. The second I see her, the knot in my stomach leaves. I jump off the bike and run to her. She wraps her arms around me and buries her face into my chest. I can feel her warmth through my shirt. I kiss her cheek. Electricity runs through my body. She pulls her head back, our eyes lock onto each other. She tilts her head – just a little. I place my lips on hers. Never have I felt so connected to another human being. I want to crawl inside of her.

"Jesus, get a room," a girl Mercedes' age says walking out the front door. "He ain't so bad lookin'. What's with the face though?" She says eying me up and down. She's dressed in short shorts and a tank top that are both two sizes too small.

"My sister Alabama," Mercedes says.

"Half-sister," Alabama corrects her.

"Possibly," Mercedes responds.

"Don't talk no trash 'bout Mom. I'll kick your ass. Done it once, do it again."

"Lets go in. My parents are both at work."

"Nice meeting you," I say, then grab the keys and backpack and follow Mercedes inside. The house smells like stale cigarettes and alcohol. Mercedes grabs my hand and leads me to the back and into her bedroom. It's like walking into a museum. Her art lines the walls. Fresh air from an open window mixed with incense fill the air.

I lean in and kiss her until we fall onto the bed. We roll over each other, taking turns on top kissing. She moves her hips into mine, I gently move mine back into hers. Again and again, we move our hips against each other – slowly. Her arms pull tighter on my back. Her hips move faster, her breathing quickens, she moans, her body quivers, and then – she's still. Her green eyes sparkle. "Your turn," she says reaching her hand down. We look into each other's eyes as her hand goes slowly up and down on me. I try to control my breathing. She breaks eye contact, lowering her green eyes below my waist. I feel her warm lips wrap around me. Her mouth moving up and down on me, her tongue spinning around me. My blood is pumping as if I'm running a marathon. I feel so alive. Her head moves faster, her lips tighten around me, until – I can't take it anymore.

We lie on our sides looking into each other's eyes.

We fall asleep.

40

A car horn wakes us up. It beeps three, four, five times – then stops. It's dark.

"My stepmom is home. You have to move the bike," Mercedes says.

We toss on clothes.

"Have you packed your stuff?" I ask.

Mercedes points to a small backpack.

"Ready," she smiles.

"What about all this?" I ask looking around her room. "Your art?"

"I'll make more. Let's get out of here."

We run out of the house. Her stepmom is in a beat up GMC with one hand on the horn and the other holding a tall can of Miller light. A cigarette hangs out of her mouth.

"Move that god damn thing or I'll run it over."

I pop the bike in neutral. "Come on. We have to back it out of here. You push on the front of the side car." Bikers always know to park so they don't have to push the bike backwards. This bike is heavy, but we get it rolling backwards onto the street. I hop on, start it, and give the throttle an extra pull. The Harley roars to life. Mercedes jumps into the sidecar.

"Bye. Bye," she laughs and we take off towards New York City.

41

NYC

After riding all night we stop and have a late breakfast at a diner in New Jersey. Next door to the diner, Mercedes finds two pairs of aviator goggles at a thrift store. They are perfect – I buy both pairs. She looks like a movie star from an old film, with her strawberry blond hair blowing out from under her skullcap and retro goggles. Her beauty is drawing a lot of attention. I can't believe how many people are taking photos of us with their phones. Every time we stop at a light, the phones point toward us. It must be the combination of two teenagers, one beautiful girl and a guy with a black eye – riding a vintage Harley Davidson with Mercedes in the sidecar on the streets of New York City.

I park the bike in a loading zone right in front of Paul White's brownstone as he suggested, and buzz his office from the locked front door. Two minutes later his assistant comes down and gives us a parking permit. "I want to do some drawing. Okay if I don't go up?" Mercedes asks.

I kiss her bye and head upstairs to meet with Paul.

An hour later I walk out the front door of Paul's building. A sea of people is standing behind the easel I bought Mercedes, as she sketches the Harley Davidson and the retail stores behind it. The drawing is beautiful. It captures the character and feel of SoHo perfectly. A woman off to her left is taking photos with an old-school camera as she sketches.

It's so cool," I tell her.

"Hey," she smiles. "I'm almost done."

I walk over to the bike and put the envelope that Paul White gave me into my pack.

"I'm going to ask and see if any of the shops across the street will buy it."

"Why? Let's keep it."

"Travel money," she says.

"How much would you like for it?" A woman in tight yoga pants and a linen shirt asks.

Mercedes freezes.

"Two hundred," I say. Mercedes looks at me like I'm nuts.

"Deal. But you have to sign it," the woman says, reaching into her purse and taking out two one hundred dollar bills. Mercedes' eyes light up. She finishes the drawing and signs it for the woman, then hands me one of the hundred dollar bills. "One for you. One for me," she says.

"No way. You earned it," I say, trying to hand it back.

She laughs and slides the bill into my front right pocket. Her hand brushes up against me. I get instantly aroused.

"Excuse me," the woman I saw taking photos says.

"May I take a few photos of the two of you? Maybe on and around your motorcycle?"

Mercedes and I look at each other.

"Why?" Mercedes asks.

"My name's Gail. I'm a writer/photographer with the *New York Times Lifestyle* magazine. I love what you drew, and come on, you are two kids on an old Harley in SoHo. Good photo op for the magazine."

I mouth the words "You want to?" to Mercedes.

"It won't take long. Promise," Gail says.

Gail has us leaning up against the bike with our arms around each other. Then she has us take turns; one of us in the sidecar while the other one is on the bike. She throws questions at us that we answer. She has us serious one minute and laughing the next. Somehow, she gets us to dance around the bike. We are having fun and I love showing off Mercedes' beauty. She has no idea how pretty she is.

"How about I buy you lunch? I'd like to do a quick interview," she explains.

"It's gotta be fast. I want to leave the city before traffic gets bad," I say.

Gail reaches into her purse and puts a press pass onto the handlebars of the bike.

"We can eat right over there so you can keep an eye on the bike. They have excellent sushi," she says pointing to a restaurant with outside seating.

42

We eat really good sushi – which is a first for Mercedes. She has only had California rolls, and has never even used chopsticks. She has trouble holding onto the sushi at first, but that doesn't affect her new love for it. She is delicate with each piece she picks up, carefully using her chopsticks and moving it to her mouth. I watch as her lips wrap around each piece and can't get over how perfect her lips are. Those same lips that were wrapped around me – the same lips that controlled me. She masters the chopsticks, and has me under her spell before we finish lunch.

Gail fires off questions the entire time we eat. She wants to know everything about our lives; how we met, where we are from. She focuses on Mercedes first and then on me. She takes notes and records the conversation on her cell phone. When Mercedes shares the story about her mom and what she has recently learned about her father, Gail's eyes fill with tears.

"I need to use the restroom. Back in two," Gail says leaving the table.

A few minutes later Gail comes back. "You don't want to get stuck in traffic and it's already started. Plus, I'd like to talk with you a little more. Listen, I just called my boss and got him to sign off on putting you up in The James Hotel," she says as if we have just won the lottery. "The hotel is right around the corner. We can get you checked in and finish this up in the lobby. You'll have the rest of the night to yourselves. And of course dinner and entertainment are on us."

"Seems like a lot of money to spend on an interview," Mercedes says.

Gail laughs.

"It would be fun to stay in the city," I say.

43

We finish up with Gail at 4:30 pm and run to our hotel room. Now, we're lying naked in bed facing each other. We were so fast at her house in North Carolina. I wanted this time to be different.

With the tip of my finger I gently trace her eyebrows, and then move down the ridge of her nose, to the crevice between her nose and lip. I circle her lips and move down her neck to her left breast. Her nipple is hard and surrounded by little bumps that I run my finger over. I take my time feeling each one. She makes a purring sound as I run my finger down her stomach to a small birthmark off to her right side. I give it my full attention, memorizing it as I circle it twice. I move to her belly button - she giggles. I kiss her there softly, and move my tongue in and around it. Her giggling stops, her upper body arches forward, her breathing increases. I leave her belly button and move my mouth below her waist. I can feel her warmth escape as I circle the outside of her with my tongue. I taste her. I increase the pressure as she did to me last night. She's pulls my hair. Her body starts to shake. She screams – then giggles.

I pull myself up, wanting nothing more in life than to make love to her. She disappears below.

"I love you," she says coming up from under the sheets.

"I love you."

My cell phone rings.

"Was I too loud?" Mercedes asks with a nervous smile.

"Was I?" I laugh and pick up the phone. "Hello."

Mercedes

I watch Nathan as he stands with the phone to his ear. He has no idea how attractive he is. Six feel tall, blond hair to his shoulders and all muscle. But lean muscle, not bulked up muscle like all the football jocks in school that were always trying to score with me. I love the way he's so calm and confident. Not afraid of anything. I saw it on the rooftop. He had no fear for his safety.

I haven't told him about the men with the black suits yet or the photos they used to blackmail me into dropping out of school.

"You want to go to a party?" He asks.

"Sure."

"Sure," He says back into the phone.

44

At least sixty guests, in their twenties, thirties and forties are at the party, and everybody is dressed in black, except me and Mercedes. She's wearing a faded yellow skirt that she bought used, and then redesigned, like all her clothes, making it a little shorter and snugger. It fits her perfectly, showing off her legs and a pair of worn-out vintage cowboy boots. She has a white V-neck sleeveless top on, which she says is made of bamboo. I have on a pair of faded jeans with holes in the knees, a white T-shirt, the thin leather jacket my mom gave me, and a pair of black flip-flops. So, I guess we stand out. "Hey, at least I have black on," I tease Mercedes.

It feels like the crowd is pretending to be having conversations, but is really checking out Mercedes. I don't blame them, and the funny thing is she's oblivious to it.

Gail walks up to us wearing a black dress. She's with a guy in his late forties with round glasses and a buzz cut. He's wearing black Converses and skinny black jeans that are way too skinny for a guy his age. "Robert, this, is Mercedes and Nathan," she says looking at us. "And, this is Robert Coldwell."

"Nice to meet you Robert," Mercedes says.

"He's with the William Morris agency," Gail says proudly.

"You're a lawyer?" I ask.

Gail and Robert laugh.

"No. We're a talent agency," he says.

"They are THE talent agency, representing some of the biggest stars of today," Gail says.

"Do you represent any painters?" I ask.

"Some of our talent are painters too. Stallone is our most famous painter."

"Cool," I say and look out the wall made of glass that separates the room we're in from the pool outside. A younger group closer to our age has come to the party and is gathered around the pool. "Hey, we're going to check out the pool. Nice to meet you Robert."

I take Mercedes' hand and as we leave I hear Robert say to Gail "They're perfect. I owe you one."

We walk out to be with the younger crowd, but they seem to be a lot like the indoor crowd – trying too hard to stand out. Mercedes and I roll our eyes at each other and start dancing. Like her brush to the canvas, she moves her body in perfect rhythm with the music. I do my best to be in sync with her, moving to the music as she does. I remember my mom saying, "If you want to really dance, you need to breathe in the music – until you feel it. I close my eyes for a minute and breathe in the music. When I open my eyes again, Mercedes and I are moving as one.

She's glowing. The entire crowd outside is dancing now. They're actually having fun. We dance until we're covered in sweat.

"Lets go swimming," Mercedes says.

"I don't have any underwear on."

"Neither do I," she smiles. "Lets show these city folk what creek swimmin' is all 'bout," she says in a fake southern accent.

"You serious?" I ask.

"I will, if you will."

I look around the party. *Come on, you'll never see these people again.* I take off my shirt, my eyes daring her to take hers off too. She does. I undo my pants, and quickly pull them off. Mercedes skirt comes off as well. "Quick!" I yell. We jump into the pool holding hands and laughing.

The music is playing, but the guys have replaced the dancing with stripping down to their underwear, and girls down to their underwear and bras. Only a few others go full Monty —but they all jump in the pool.

It's as if none of us have ever been in a pool before. We are all giggling and splashing. People are swimming under water, doing breaststrokes between each other's legs. I go underwater to do the same and swim towards Mercedes open legs. I take three strokes and it all comes back.

"What's wrong?" Mercedes looks at me like she's scared.

"Nothing."

"You're pale white."

"It's just – Listen, I don't want a pity party. But this is the first time I've been in the water since the accident. The second, actually. I tried drowning myself, Mercedes, two days after I lost Mom and Dad." Just saying it to someone else makes me feel better.

"Oh Nathan. I'm so sorry. I never should have suggested swimming."

"I'm glad you did. Really. I'm good now. I've let it go," I say pulling her close for a kiss.

"You can't let something like that go so quickly."

"Yes, you can."

She leans forward, her green eyes sparkling, and kisses me. I kiss her back until I've forgotten everything but my love for her.

"Lets go," I hear her whisper in my ear.

"Yea," I say looking down. "But I need a minute to… hmmm."

"To think of anything other than me kissing you?" She smiles.

45

Mercedes

For two nights now, we've been staying at the Courtyard Marriott in Hudson Falls, NY, under Nathan's dad's business account. We ride into town every morning at 7am and have breakfast at a diner that's full of locals who keep to themselves.

When I wake up the first morning, Nathan is sitting on a chair, across from the bed doing his meditation. He sits perfectly still but has tears coming down his cheeks. Twenty minutes later when he is done, I ask him "What is it?"

"I had a moment with my mom. She was telling me, telling us – to be careful. I know that sounds like new age crap, but it felt real."

"If it felt real, it was real. Will you teach me – to meditate?"

"Of course."

"How long have you been doing it?"

My parents taught me how to do it in fifth grade to help

ground me. I was a hyper mess."

"You hyper? I find that hard to believe."

"Up until the accident I was up at five every morning, I meditated twice a day, and exercised at least an hour a day. I need that routine to feel normal – so my head won't explode."

"Then get back at it. I'll paint while you exercise," and that's what we do.

I set up my easel close to the cliff's edge, looking out over the Hudson River with Garrison, NY on the far side and West Point, the country's top military academy – according to the locals, on our side. I want to capture every detail – the river, the town, the school, the students in uniform, and the action as they march from class to class.

Nathan does yoga and a variety of exercises the entire time I paint. He moves like a tiger hunting its prey as he goes from one exercise to another. When he finishes he is calm and a lot more fun to be around.

The last morning in town we head back to the local diner for breakfast, but this time the locals eye us suspiciously. When we finish, we walk up to pay the cashier.

"It's on me kids. You stay strong. Ride safe." She looks like she is about to cry as she speaks.

"That was weird," Nathan says once we're outside the restaurant. "Nice of her – but weird".

"Yeah, the whole vibe was different this morning," I say.

46

Nathan

We're on the bike headed north to Saratoga Springs, where I had Paul White get Rusty a room in a rehab. There is no doubt in my mind that Rusty is sorry for what happened in the hotel room. You can't act sorry — he was, and he knew he needed help. I had Paul post his bail, get him a lawyer, and find him a top rehab close by. I know deep in my heart he's a good guy and I still want to help him.

Two hours later we're sitting in the lobby of the rehab waiting for Rusty. People keep walking in and out. They all smile at us. Some say hi. It's weird.

"Well, if it isn't the celebrities of the hour," Rusty says. "Mercedes. Nice to meet you."

He already looks much healthier. How is that possible? He's only been here a short time.

"What's going on in here? You look great," I say.

"Sobriety, kid."

"Congratulations," Mercedes says as a woman walks into the lobby, looks at us and walks back out.

"What's with all the people coming in and out of here?" I ask.

"Yeah, it's a little weird," Mercedes says.

"You're celebrities – get used to it."

"What are you talking about?" I ask.

"You haven't seen it?"

"Seen what?"

Rusty walks over to the table in the middle of the lobby and grabs the Life Style magazine out of the *NY Times* and holds it up. On the front page is a full-page photo of Mercedes and me leaning against the Harley Davidson in SoHo.

"What the heck," I say looking at the photo.

I thought we were getting a lot of attention riding up here," Mercedes says as she opens the magazine to the article. "My god, its six pages long."

"That's why the cars were flashing their lights and beeping their horns?" I exclaim, looking at her.

"It's actually eight pages – continued in the back," Rusty is glowing.

I hadn't really thought about it, about letting Gail take a few photos for a blurb in a magazine – but man, these are full-page professional photos.

"That's one hell of a cool photo on the cover, kid. I may have to get a signed copy for my wall."

"Let's get some lunch," I suggest.

On the walk to the restaurant I remember a conversation I overheard my dad have about reporters. *Don't say anything to a reporter unless you want it published.* Mercedes and I told Gail everything. She was like a friend asking us what was going on in our lives. She talked about her teenage years, and then asked about ours. I'd even forgotten it was an interview.

"Guess people still read newspapers," I say – more to myself then to them.

47

We're at a small restaurant on Main Street. Rusty and Mercedes are sitting across from me. Television sets line the walls, one hanging directly behind them. I work hard not to watch it.

I still can't get over the transformation Rusty has had. His entire being is different. He even orders a salad.

"You look good Rusty. You look happy," I say, still distracted by the TV.

"Longest I've been without booze or dope."

"Congratulations," Mercedes says.

"Thanks. I feel like I might be able to do it this time. I owe it to him."

"Nathan. What is it? What's the matter?" Mercedes asks.

The news is showing Senator Grant walking up to a ballot box. I can't hear the audio but I can read the copy. *Senator Grant, the biggest opponent of the pipeline, did a one-eighty this morning*

161

voting for the project, making his vote the deciding factor in our country's biggest pipeline to date. The environmentalists are in an uproar. Protesters are already lining up outside his office calling him a traitor. Construction for the pipeline starts in two weeks.

"I forgot all about it."

"About what?" Mercedes asks.

"The thumb drive." I'm still staring at the TV. "The day before we got hit by the storm, before my parents died. I forgot all about it."

"What about the thumb drive?" Rusty asks.

I told them about Dad connecting to the Russian satellite, about how nervous he was when I walked in on him, what the information was capable of doing, and about the politicians, CEO's and professional athletes that were on the thumb drives. The criminal activities, the affairs, the secrets, and compromising situations they were all caught in.

"I've got the thumb drive in my pack," I whisper. "I haven't looked at it, but I saw the photo of Senator Grant in bed with two teenage Thai boys. The Russians must have a stake in the pipeline."

"Why would the Russians want more oil coming into America from Canada?" Rusty asks himself more than me.

"It's all on the thumb drive?" Mercedes asks.

"Yes," I whisper. "I pressed Dad for more details. He said the photo I saw was just the tip of the iceberg, and the information is probably already changing the direction of America. He told me if we got caught with the photos we'd have Russian and U.S.

government agencies after us until they destroyed us."

The three of us sat in silence.

"We need to look at the thumb drive," Rusty says looking at me.

"Yeah. But we'll need a computer. My iPad doesn't take thumb drives."

"We can go to the library," Mercedes says.

"No, we can't use a public computer. We'll have to buy one."

The waitress puts the check down in front of Rusty and turns to Mercedes. "Loved the photos of you two online. God bless you two."

48

Saratoga Springs is an upscale historic town – old and new money mixed together. It's also home to the Saratoga Race Track and Skidmore College, a small liberal arts school. Mercedes and I are walking down Main Street, nodding to strangers that acknowledge us, and most do – and it's freaky. The photos from the article went viral. We're all over the Internet and the news. A couple in their thirties holding a Maltese puppy ask if they can have their photo taken with us.

"What's with the cold shoulder?" Mercedes asks after the couple leaves.

A group of students from Skidmore walk up to us, all holding their phones out to take pictures. "Nathan, Mercedes," the lead guy says wearing a Skidmore sweatshirt and sounding like he's our best friend. "You guys want to get high?"

"We don't get high," I say.

"How about some beers then?"

Mercedes steps in front of me. "Thank you for the offer but we have plans," she smiles and takes my hand, leading me into the first store.

"So what's your deal?"

"I'm good."

"No you're not."

I take a moment, slowly inhaling and exhaling.

"Nothing. I'm good."

"You're not good, Nathan, you've been standoffish to me all afternoon."

"Really, its nothing. I'm good."

"You're not good. You're being a shit."

I didn't run this morning and my mind has been racing all day. Mom kept pounding into me how exercising was essential for controlling my hyper activity. "It's your choice, exercise every morning or go on medication," she'd say. Right now, I wish I were on medication because my head feels like it's going to explode.

"You want to break up?" she asks me.

"What?"

"It's fine, Nathan. Just tell me. I'll go back home."

Hearing her words stops my racing thoughts and focuses me.

"The thumb drive could destroy us." I say looking at her for what feels like the first time all day. "We can travel anywhere we want. We can do anything we want. Break up? No. I don't want to lose you. I love you."

We kiss.

"I fell in love with you the moment I saw you. Nothing is going to destroy us," she says.

"If we decide to go public with the photos, we'd probably be on the run forever. You wouldn't be able to meet your biological dad. You wouldn't be able to sell your artwork."

"You've been saying I should start running," she smiles.

"It's not a joke," I say, trying not to laugh.

She pulls me closer. "You're all I care about. Why don't we look at the drive and then decide if we want to go public with it. And if we go public with it, we'll cover our tracks. Now come on." She pulls my hand, leading me out of the store. "Let's forget about it until tomorrow and go have some fun."

49

We check into the Saratoga Springs Courtyard Marriott, and the second we walk into the room, we rip each other's clothes off. I push Mercedes against the wall, and put a hand on each side of her shoulders, locking her in place. I stare into her eyes. "You're mine." With my left hand I lift her chin and kiss her. She kisses me back. I pick her up, carry her towards the bed, and then I throw her onto the comforter. She lands on her back. I grab her ankles and pull them quickly until she's at the edge of the bed. I drop to my knees putting my head between her legs, and make love to her with my tongue. Her fingers pull on my hair. Her body quivers. I want to make love to her. I want to be inside of her. I pull myself onto the bed. She wraps her legs around me. I can feel her warmth as we rub against each other. Her body has beads of sweat escaping from her pores. I slip my index finger into her, moving it slowly in and around her. She reaches down with her hand and performs magic. I've lost control of my breathing. She has too. My toes start to curl. My body shivers. We pass out.

50

Mercedes

The sun coming in through the window blinds wakes me up. It's 6:30 am according to the clock on the bedside table. I roll over and see Nathan in the corner of the room doing his meditation. I'm so happy he's back into his routine. I say a quick prayer. "Thank you for bringing Nathan into my life, thank you for all you have given me," and slip out of bed and into the shower.

Feeling refreshed from my shower, I put the terry cloth robe with the Marriott logo on and walk back into the room. Nathan's upside down, in a headstand, balancing on his elbows and forearms. I laugh and watch as he pushes himself up from the headstand into a full handstand, balances for a minute, and then flips onto his feet. I get goose bumps.

"I've got it," he says.

"Yes, you do," I smile. He looks at me quizzically. Then smiles back as if he's figured out my thoughts.

"We're going to give the thumb drive to Rusty. He can look at it first if he wants to. But we're going to stick with our plan and ride across the country to meet your dad. We'll meet up with Rusty in Stockton after his rehab."

"You trust him that much?"

"I don't know. I think so. He's a good guy that made some bad choices. He's got a big heart, though. I saw it in his eyes after he chased me down on the highway. Plus, what's the worst that can happen?"

"He could give it to someone or sell it."

"It wouldn't affect us if he did. Maybe we'll get lucky and he'll loose it," Nathan laughs. "I want to have fun, Mercedes. I want to meet your dad, and explore the world with you."

"I like that idea."

"I do too. We'll have a few weeks of fun before we decide what to do with the photos on the drive," he says.

I open my robe, standing naked in front of him. "Lets start now."

We're standing outside a stone church on Main street, waiting for Rusty's AA meeting to finish up. The side door opens, and dozens of people walk outside; some are smiling, some are laughing, and a few look sad. Rusty is one of the last to come out. He's talking with a guy that looks down and out. I can hear him say, "Everything is going to be okay if you take it a day at a time." He pats the guy on the shoulder and walks over to us.

"Nice disguise," he says, laughing at our baseball caps pulled low to our sunglasses.

"Hey, so far it's been working," Nathan says as he hands him the envelope with the thumb drive and says "Look at it if you want to, but make sure your not connected to the Internet if you do. We can meet up at your house when you're finished with the rehab and after Mercedes gets to spend some time with her dad. There's some cash in there for you to get home."

Rusty shakes his head. "I don't know what to say other then thanks. I owe you." Rusty hugs first Nathan, then me. "You two ride safe."

51

Rusty

Fuck. Fuck. Fuck. Focus. Fuck. Focus, goddamn it. "God fucking damn it!" I yell.

The door to my room opens up "Russ, what's going on? You all right?" Gary, the morning auditor asks.

"Yeah," I say.

"You look like dog crap."

"Didn't sleep much."

"Where's Jimmy?" Gary looks at the empty bed across from mine.

"I'm not his sitter."

"Was he here last night?"

"I'm not his sitter, Gary. And I'm not a nark." I try not to take my rage out on Gary. Without him, I would have left this place the first morning. Sitting around bitching about the past isn't something I wanted to be a part of. Gary pulled me aside after the first meeting and told me *"Maintaining sobriety is a constant*

175

struggle in the beginning. You'll experience a lot of emotional tur-moil. Just play along for today. Pretend to enjoy the process. "

"Get some breakfast. Group meets in half an hour," he says glancing around the room quickly like a detective, and then walks out.

My rage has nothing to do with sobriety. I wish I could tell him – tell anyone to help relieve the pressure building in my brain. My first tour in Iraq, three of my buddies blew up next to me from a roadside bomb. A guy on the second floor balcony across the street smiled as he put his cell phone into his pocket. I was covered with blood – none of it mine. A surge of energy fueled my body and mind. Rage. I dropped my pack, ran across the street, and smashed my shoulder into the front door, splinters of wood from the smashed door were still in the air, as I lifted my pistol, and shot the first man I saw. He was walking out of an apartment door, then went flying back in from the force of the bullet, and landed in front of three screaming kids. A woman ran into the room, something in her hand, a gun – I went to pull the trigger – it was a spatula. The pistol fired, but my instincts had kicked in and moved the pistol just enough, the spatula fell from her hand, the bullet hit the wall over her shoulder. I kept moving, taking the stairs three at a time, and rounded the corner on the second floor to the only door, that would lead to the balcony. I flipped my M4 rifle off my shoulder. Pointed it at the door – and pulled on the trigger as I walked closer. I moved my arms back and forth, spraying the area until the magazine was empty. The door had flown off the hinges. I snapped another magazine into the M4 and walked toward the opening. The only sounds were from my boots. I stopped walking. I heard a whimper. Blood dripped off my forehead into my left eye. I went to wipe it off and see bone fragments stuck to my shirt. Fuel. I lifted the M4 and walked into the room. Time stood still. In my peripheral vision I saw bombs, suicide vests, and weapons. Directly in front of me stood the man from the balcony. He was holding a remote control. Sitting in front of him were a woman and teenage boy. I could see the hate in their eyes.

"Stand back or I blow us up!" he yelled.

I took a step forward – my gun pointed at his head.

"Back. Back. Get back. I push the button. We all die."

"I guess we're all going to die then," I said, taking another step forward and moving my gun down to the boy and pulling the trigger, and watched as his head cracked open.

The terrorist's hands were shaking over the button as he screamed, "Stop. Stop. Stop. I push the button. We all die."

The woman next to the headless boy was wailing in prayer.

I moved the gun to her and pulled the trigger; the wailing stopped.

"Push the button! Push the button. You Goddamned coward, "I screamed.

He dropped to his knees in prayer. I held the trigger down, letting the bullets fly out, and watched as his body parts covered the back wall. When the magazine was empty, I picked up the remote control, closed my eyes, and pushed the button. Rage was not my friend. The remote malfunctioned.

That was then. This is now. Rage still isn't my friend, but I'm going to get a grip on it. Last night, I used my roommate's laptop to look at the thumb drive. What I found –I'm still trying to process. My son is in prison for life for killing a cop. He swore he had been set up by the governor of California. Crystal meth has a way of damaging the brain and leading addicts to believe their own twisted fantasies. He got clean two months before the trial, but still kept up with his story about the governor. We all knew he was guilty – the prosecutor, the jury, his sister and I. I'm not a fan of cops, most bikers aren't, but this cop was a good guy. He did a lot of charity work for inner city youth. He stood up against police brutality. The jury took less then an hour to find my son guilty of all charges. They knew what I knew – he was guilty.

But this thumb drive has photos of the governor of California, the governor that made his fortune in real estate, accepting bags of cash from police officers, sport promoters and pimps. Was my son innocent? Did the governor set him up so he could get the cop off the streets? I have to find out, and in order to do that, I have to control the rage.

I promised Nathan I wouldn't tell anyone about the thumb drive. But this can't wait. It's not just my son – it's my brothers too. Last year, three brothers from the club were put away on trumped up drug charges. They all got twenty to life – they all said they were set up. So last night I downloaded three photos of the governor: one with the owner of the Oakland Raiders and two guys in black suits handing him a bag of cash, one with the Mexican cartel handing him hefty bags full of cash, and one of the governor giving briefcases full of cash to four policemen.

I opened a Yahoo account under my roommate's name and sent the three photos to the *New York Times, LA Times, CNN, FOX News, the Huffington Post* and *Politico*. Then, this morning, I sent them out to a bunch of blogs.

My roommate, Jimmy, isn't a good guy. He spends every night bragging about having sex with underage girls and talking about how fucked up he's going to get once he leaves rehab. The judge waved his six-month jail sentence for a hit-and-run if he completes rehab, and his parents promised him a large inheritance if he completes the program. He's a three-time loser, and I have no problem leaving an electronic paper trail from the photos back to him.

I take the six hundred dollars from the envelope that Nathan gave me, put it in my pocket and look up at the calendar on the wall. "Fourteen days, and twelve hours of sobriety," I say to myself. "I can do this," I walk out of rehab taking my rage with me, one step at a time.

Nathan had preached to me and Mercedes that privacy is non-existent today. "If you shop online or own a smartphone, every move, every action, every conversation you have is recorded, documented and stored on servers across the country. The stories you read online, the stuff you buy, places you go. It's all documented, traded, sold and stored. The only way you can have one hundred percent privacy today is to live off the grid," he told us. Like most, I believe our privacy is limited, but not to the extent that Nathan believes. Then again, he and Mercedes only use their phones for calls, GPS, quick research. Neither of them uses a social network.

52

"I'll need a photo ID," the woman behind the Amtrak counter says to me.

"I'm paying cash," I tell her.

"Patriot act. ID for all travel. Got to keep America safe," she says without looking up.

I hand her my military ID.

"Four-day trip with layovers," she says glancing at my ID "Three hundred seventy-five for a seat, seven hundred for a sleeper car."

I hand her four one hundred dollar bills.

Using Nathan's earlier advice, I sit down to meditate. It's not easy. Shit flies around my brain as I repeat the mantra "peaceful" to myself. *Taking advice from an eighteen-year-old? Peaceful. Peaceful. What's he doing? What's my son doing? Peaceful. Peaceful. Peaceful. Meditation is a crock of shit, Peaceful.*

Peaceful. Is it working? Peaceful. Peaceful. Peaceful. Peaceful. Peaceful. Peaceful.

"Can I get you something to drink?" a woman's voice asks as I open my eyes.

"What time is it?"

"One-thirty," she says.

My God. One hour has gone by. It works. My head is clear.

"We have beer, and mixed drinks."

"Soda?" I ask looking up at her. She's looks around fifty-five, a little overweight like me, and wrinkles that show a life lived fast and hard, like me.

She smiles and in a flirtatious way and says, "We have Coke, Diet Coke, ice tea, orange crush, and Dr. Pepper."

"No seltzer?"

"And seltzer."

"I'll take a seltzer with a lime."

"Had you pegged for a Bud guy."

"Sober."

"Hell yeah." She glows. "Me too. How long you got?"

"Fourteen days. How about you?"

"I went to bed sober. I woke up sober," she laughs, then starts to cough, and in a raspy voice says, "One day at a time."

She hands me the seltzer. "Thanks Zephoria?" I say, reading from her name tag.

"Leslie, but friends call me Liz. I left my tag at home."

"Friends call me Rusty."

"Russell?"

"Do I look like a Russell?"

"You look like a biker." Her smile is contagious.

Well, Liz, how much do I owe you for the seltzer?"

"It's on me. How far you going Rusty?"

"Stockton," I say, leaning into the center aisle to see if anyone is within earshot. I pull a hundred dollar bill from my pocket and place it in Liz's hand. "This is yours if you can sneak me a sleeper car for the trip," I whisper to her.

She doesn't hesitate. "We have two rooms down for repair. She slips the bill into her front pocket. "I'll even bring you food. Just don't you get drunk and get me fired."

"I promise not to," I say as she pushes the beverage cart down the aisle.

"Oh, and you have to promise to take me for a ride on the coast this summer."

"I would like that," I tell her.

53

"T o l e d o," the loudspeaker blares, waking me up. My body feels glued to the mattress. I had no idea a train's bed could be so comfortable. That was the best night's sleep I've ever had.

Knock. Knock.

"Yeah," I yell.

"Two hour layover Rusty. If you need anything, get it now," Liz says from outside the door.

I hop into the shower and make a mental list of things I want to buy in town – a pad of paper, pens, colored markers, pencils and erasers.

54

Nathan

West of Ohio, there is little for us to do, other then ride fast, stop for gas, use the bathroom, and buy more food. So we make good time to California, and Mercedes' excitement grows the closer we get to Malibu. After leaving Rusty we found out her dad was teaching at Pepperdine University in Malibu and we are headed out to meet him.

"Hi dad. What have you been up to, Dad? Ehhhhh. Okay, I'm still nervous. But I'm happy. I'm happy I'm going to meet my dad," she says looking at me.

We're now twenty miles outside of Los Angeles going seventy miles an hour in bumper-to-bumper traffic, and cars are going nuts, flashing their lights, swerving towards us. Drivers giving us the thumbs up or peace sign. Passengers lean out of their windows yelling our names, and trying to touch the bike. It's unreal. Why would anyone want this kind of attention?

Welcome to Los Angeles. Mercedes points to the sign on the side of the 101 freeway.

I pull off the freeway and stop at a 7-Eleven for gas

"That was stressful," I say, taking off my skull cap.

"It was crazy. I need to go to use the restroom. What do you want from inside?" Mercedes asks, taking off her helmet. She's even more beautiful covered in sweat and road dust.

"Surprise me," I say, watching her walk away in her faded jeans and white tank top. I push my Amex card into the slot, select high test and start filling the tank. Driving long distance has mellowed me out. *Mom and Dad would be proud of me for taking this trip across country.*

This bike is totally their style.

"Can we get a picture?"

I feel a hand on my shoulder.

"Hey, can we get a picture?" Two girls my age in skintight shorts and shirts that leave little to the imagination ask.

I try not to stare, but they look like mannequins in a department store. Too perfect – too fake. With one on each side of me, they put an arm over my shoulder and kiss my cheeks. "You're so hot," one says as they click away with their phones.

"Okay, that's good," I tell them when I feel one of their hands move down the back of my shorts.

"Your so rad, Nathan."

"Mercedes. We follow you guys on Facebook!" they yell as she walks towards us with two ice teas.

"I'm not on Facebook," Mercedes says.

"Your fan page. I'm on your fan page."

All of a sudden a group of people surrounds the bike. Everyone of them young, and dressed like they're on the cover of the magazines you see at checkout counters. I feel claustrophobic. I nod my head to Mercedes and get on the bike as she gets in the sidecar.

"We gotta go. Nice meeting you," I say, starting the bike and pulling away from the island of gas pumps.

"Nathan, watch out!" Mercedes yells.

I was looking over my shoulder and didn't see an SUV fly into the parking lot. I slam on the breaks, stopping the bike an inch from the front bumper. Two guys jump out leaving the doors open. One has a TMZ baseball cap on and is holding a microphone. The other guy is holding a video camera. I see the recording light on.

I take a deep breath. "Please move your car."

The cameraman gets right in Mercedes' face.

"So did you bang the football player on the roof or not?" he asks.

I take my helmet off. My fingers tingle. My heart beats faster. I slow my breathing. I stare at the cameraman. He's probably pissed off actors, he's probably been pushed, kicked, and has had some punches thrown at him, but those were probably for show. This was going to be a different experience for him.

I hold my stare. "Apologize!"

"Well, give us your answer," he smirks, looking back at Mercedes, and doesn't see me reach for his wrist until I have it. I pull him hard into me, and flip him over my left shoulder. He lands on his back – the camera beside him, I reach down and pop the memory card from it and slip it in my pocket.

"Apologize!"

"Okay, okay. I'm sorry," his eyes full of pain and bewilderment.

"Wow. Yeah. Kick his ass!" I turn towards the yelling. A wall of people, they are cheering.

"That was so hot," one of the girls yells.

Totally rad," the other joins in.

I push the bike and sidecar backwards a few feet so we can get around the SUV.

"Let's go," I say hopping back on the bike. We take off for the 10 freeway.

"Are you okay?" I look down at Mercedes.

"Yes," she says, shaking her head side to side – and from what my dad had told me, it's a subconscious thing people do, without even realizing it, when they say yes but what they really mean is no. "That was insane," she yells over the engine as we pick up speed.

"We've got to lose the bike and get a car," I yell back.

"But I love this bike."

"I know. Me too."

55

Pepperdine College sits high on a hill in Malibu, overlooking the Pacific Ocean. To call it beautiful is an understatement. I pull the bike up to the security gate, "You're here for Jean Phillip Martin," the guard says. "Yes. How did you know?" I ask.

"The whole country knows," he laughs and puts a walkie-talkie to his mouth. "The Dynamic Duo is here." He looks at his watch, writes the time down on a sheet of paper, and then smiles at us. "Head up to building 4. You'll know when you get there."

"Thank you." The gate opens and we head up a perfectly paved steep road that twists back and forth. "They don't need to worry about plowing here," I say trying to lighten the mood.

We ride the bike around the last corner, and smack in front of building 4 is a large CBS truck. I look down at Mercedes as I park the bike and take off my skullcap. She's not smiling.

A woman in her twenties, professionally dressed, comes

running out of building 4 and meets us as we get off the bike.

"Welcome to Pepperdine," she says. I'm Sally Cross, the administrative director. We are so excited you're here, Mercedes. You too, Nathan." Mercedes looks at me, her eyes full of emotional turmoil.

We follow Sally inside the front door. Two large tables are set up, one with film equipment, one with a lot of food. A side door opens up, "Nathan, Mercedes. Finally. I've been worried. What the hell took you so long? No, don't worry about it. You're here now," Robert, the guy from the pool party, Gail's friend, the agent, says.

"What are you doing here? What the hell's happening? I ask him.

"Babe, you two have been on every network, every website, every goddamn chat room. You're bigger than the Kardashians ever were. You're huge. You're stars. Every network wanted this deal. It was a bidding war. CBS won the exclusive. I just need you two to sign some paperwork first." Robert is glowing.

"We're here to see her father, that's it. We don't want a deal. You should go back to NY."

Robert laughs, "Mercedes, your father has already signed. Guys, this is going to be the biggest network special since man landed on the moon. You're going to get two hundred fifty thousand for this, and a first class trip to Paris so you can meet all your relatives," he says looking at Mercedes, who looks like she just saw a ghost.

"He signed the papers?" Her voice breaking as she asks Robert.

"Let's go, Robert," a walkie-talkie attached to Robert's belt blares out.

"What was that?" Robert looks at Mercedes.

"Let's get out of here," tears fill Mercedes' eyes, she grabs my hand, and we run out of the building. I hear Robert screaming, but have no idea what he's saying as we hop on the bike and take off down the hill, going as fast as I dare without flipping the bike over, headed towards the Pacific Coast Highway.

After a few miles I pull off the PCH onto a side road to park the bike, but at the end of the road I see a beautiful shingled hotel that looks like it should be on Cape Cod instead of in California. I look down at Mercedes in the sidecar and point to the hotel. Her face is marked with tear streaks. "Okay," she says trying to smile.

I pull in front of the hotel and see a sign for an underground lot off to the right that says *Private parking. Staff only.* I pull into the underground lot and park the bike.

"Did I foul up? That's a lot of money," Mercedes asks.

"My God, don't worry about the money – I told you, we don't need money."

"Nathan. That's a quarter of a million dollars. Obviously, my dad doesn't give a crap about me. I should have taken the money."

"Come on." I say grabbing her backpack from the bike. "Grab my pack. I'll take yours."

Mercedes looks at me to see if I'm serious. My pack is heavy, and three times the size of hers.

"Come on. Move. Lets go inside before any paparazzi sees us," I say, trying to sound pissed off.

Mercedes picks up my pack, struggles to put on the shoulder straps, and starts walking out of the garage. "What's this? One of your emotional tricks to snap me out of this? Well, it's not going to work. My dad just sold me off for a quarter of a million dollars. Unlike you, I think it's okay to be sad when your own family fucks you over! We could have used that money, Nathan," she turns to me – sees me smiling. She looks like she might attack.

I stop smiling, put both my hands up, palms forward. "You already have half a million dollars."

"What?"

"You have half a million dollars," I smile, and nod towards the pack.

"In cash. There is half a million dollars in the bottom of that backpack, Mercedes. Actually, a few thousand less, but close enough. I told you, we don't need money. I'm rich, which means you're rich. My dad owned the top Internet security firm in the country. We don't need money – you don't need money. If you still want to meet your dad, we'll meet your dad. But please, don't do it for the money."

"You've been leaving this in the hotel rooms when we go out. Didn't you worry about it?"

"Dirty underwear on top, who's going to go through that?"

56

The front desk employee told us the hotel has a strict privacy policy, and is used by celebrities, politicians, and others because they know they won't be bothered when they stay at here. She checks us in and doesn't mention that she knows who we are. "Enjoy your privacy," she says, which is exactly what I want to hear as she hands back my ID and American Express card.

We follow the bellman to the elevators, passing a table full of newspapers: *USA Today,* the *Los Angeles Times, the New York Times* and *The Wall Street Journal*. With the exception of *The Wall Street Journal,* Mercedes and I are on all the other covers. *New York Times*: "Dynamic Duo takes the country by storm." *LA Times*: "The Dynamic Duo rides into our hearts." *USA Today*: "Dynamic Duo ignites passion." I grab a copy of each and hide them under my arm.

"It's pretty wild, huh?" the bellman says.

"Please don't bring it up to anyone, I mean that we're staying here," I say.

"No worries. We all sign a confidentiality form. Plus, I'm putting myself through school, and the money's good here. We get celebrities all the time, and if any of us leak who is staying – we get fired on the spot, and fined. You're good here," he says, raising his eyebrows.

"Thanks," Mercedes says as he opens the door to our room. "Wow. This is beautiful," she smiles for the first time.

The entire front wall of the room is glass and looks out over the Pacific Ocean. One large and two small windows are opened a crack, letting in the sound of the rolling waves, and the smell of salt from the ocean.

"It's perfect," I say holding her hand.

"Anything you need, just call down to the front desk, or you can also use the TV," he says, pointing to the television that's already turned on showing the hotel's features. My name is Jason, I can get you just about anything if it's legal, and some things that aren't," he laughs.

"Thanks. We're all set," I say handing him a twenty-dollar bill from my front pocket. "Thank you." He walks out.

"I'm so tired," Mercedes says, sitting on the edge of the bed.

"Me too. You want me to shut the shades so we can take a nap?" I ask.

"No, just turn off the TV."

I walk over to the bedside table, grab the remote and push the first red button I see. Instead of the TV turning off, it switches to the news. A reporter is walking up to the front door of a small white house – the front door of Mercedes' house in NC.

"You've got to be kidding," Mercedes says.

The front door opens just enough to see the man she grew up believing to be her father.

"I told you people to stop coming by. I don't want your god-damn money. I want to know if my daughter is safe. Is she okay? Can you tell me that?" he asks, with black bags under his eyes.

"If we do find her, what would you like us to tell her?" the woman holding the mike asks.

Cracking the door open a little more – he leans out.

"Baby girl. I tried my best. I loved your mom so much. I love you so much. I always have. You're your mom's little girl. A replica. I tried my best, but the older you got, the more you looked like her, and it kept breaking my heart. I knew about the affair, she was devastated when she found out he didn't care for her. She was so young. We both were. Mercedes, when your mom died – I died. Go live your life. Be safe." He shuts the door.

Mercedes is trying to hold it together. I sit next to her and put my arm around her shoulders.

"I'm so confused," she says.

I want to say something. Anything, but have no idea what would help.

"What kind of man accepts money to meet his daughter for the first time? I was so excited to meet him. I need to call my dad – my real dad," she looks at me, tears dripping down the sides of her face, "not my biological prick dad."

Mercedes digs her phone out of her pack to call home when the news cuts to another reporter, a man my dad's age sitting at a desk. On the bottom of the screen in red letters it reads, *"Breaking news – The Dynamic Duo has hit Los Angeles"*. The reporter looks up from a monitor on his desk, "this just in – the dynamic duo has hit the streets of LA, and not without controversy – trouble seems to following these two. Is Nathan protecting Mercedes?" He pauses for dramatic effect. "Or has his sudden celebrity status gone to his head?" Another pause. "You decide." The screen cuts to the 7-Eleven we were at earlier.

"Shit," I say.

A perfect video of us pulling into the gas station, Mercedes going into the store, me pumping gas, the kiss from the girls. Me flipping the camera man and taking the card out of the camera. It cuts to one of the girls that kissed me. "He was rad. totally rad, that dude was in Mercedes' face – camera actually hit her, he got so close. Follow me, Nathan, instragirl199," she yells.

They cut to an older man, "the camera guy blocked them in," he says.

They cut to a heavyset woman holding the hands of two children, "My kids are traumatized by all this violence, we need some compensation, that's right. Compensation!" she yells at the camera.

"Where's the remote?" I ask, forgetting I still have it in my hand. I start to raise it to the TV to turn it off.

"Mercedes, I've spent a lifetime seeking you out. My dear, dear, Mercedes, please. Come to France and meet your family." It cuts back to the reporter. "That was Mercedes' biological father, a French artist and professor here at —." I shut the TV off.

57

Rusty

It feels good to walk around after a good, sober night's sleep. I pick up the pace, swing my arms a little more, raise my knees a little higher, and then start laughing at what I must look like in my biker jacket, and long hair, power walking down the street. Fuck it, I don't care, I feel good. I pick up the pace even more.

Half an hour later I circle back to the station and go inside for a cup of coffee and to see if the train is still on schedule. The station is one large room with gates lining one wall and vendors the other. A small crowd of people is standing in front of a television set, footage of a large fire and a street with nothing but smoldering foundations fill the screen. It looks oddly familiar. The volume is turned high. I walk closer as a news helicopter flying over the fire zooms in on it. "Two full blocks of Saratoga Springs, NY have exploded, leveling the area, and killing hundreds. Police say it could take months to find out the exact number of casualties. A gas leak is thought to be the cause," the commentator says.

"Mother fucker," I say to no one.

I leave the station, and walk a few blocks to a barbershop I had passed on my power walk. I get a buzz cut and have my beard shaved off. I look and feel ten years younger.

I pick up a disposable phone and head back to the train. Once I'm in my room, I strip down to my boxers, not a pretty sight, and do some calisthenics: burpees, push-ups and leg lifts. I'm overweight, but once a soldier always a soldier – muscle memory doesn't forget. I have a mission and a new lease on life.

58

Nathan

Mercedes and I are in the garage of the hotel with Jason, the bellman who checked us in. This morning, the paparazzi were outside the front doors of the hotel, waiting for Mercedes and me to go outside. Last night, one of the guests had seen me walk into the gift shop where I had bought Mercedes a present. Apparently, the guest sold our whereabouts to the highest bidder.

I hand Jason the keys to the Harley – he hands me two baseball caps; one with an LA Rams logo, one with a Venice beach logo, "let me know when you want this back. I'll treat it right," he says smiling at the bike. Then, he looks back at us and says, "Jocko did a good job with you two. "

Jason hooked us up with Jocko, the hotel's head stylist, this morning. He was exactly what we needed. He was flamboyant, positive, and hysterical. He gave Mercedes a Bob Cut, dyed her hair black, and gave her a box of brown contact lenses. He gave me a buzz cut.

"You sure you don't want to sit in the front seat with Jason? No one is going to recognize you," I tell her.

"And miss the fun?" she says, taking the hat with the Venice beach logo and putting it on her head. Of course, it looks fantastic.

"You're too darn pretty," I tell her. "Let's see the glasses," she puts on the non-prescription, black glasses that Jocko gave her. "Who are you?" I ask her, as Jason opens the trunk to the ten-year-old black Volkswagen Jetta he traded for a Harley with a sidecar.

We climb into the trunk, and feel each bump as Jason drives us out of the hotel and onto the PCH. Five minutes later the car stops and Jason lets us out of the trunk, handing us the keys.

59

We've been driving north on the PCH for two hours, each lost in our own thoughts.

"I'm really going to miss that bike," Mercedes says.

I look over at this beautiful brunette, and feel as if I'm cheating on Mercedes. "Me too."

"Where are we going?"

"I have an idea."

My phone rings, I don't recognize the number but answer it anyway.

"Hello," I say.

"You watch the news?" Rusty asks.

We've been trying not to.

"Change of plans. We have less then a minute to talk. They blew up the Rehab. Blew up two full blocks of Saratoga

Springs."

"What are you talking about?" I ask

"Your dad was right. I'm headed home." The line goes dead.

I turn off my cell phone and take a minute to digest what Rusty just told me.

"Give me your phone," I say to Mercedes. "He told someone."

I pull the car over to the side of the road, and with the closest rock, I smash our iPhones to pieces then get back into the car.

"Don't you think you're being a bit paranoid?" Mercedes asks as we drive off.

I toss a handful of pieces out the window. "Once the government or a well-run gang gets inside your phone, your iPad, your computer - they own you. You'll be watched, listened to, and tracked. No, it's not paranoia – it's reality."

"So, are we officially on the run?"

"I hope not," I say, and throw a few more pieces of our cell phones out the window and start to giggle. "This is the second time I've deliberately polluted."

"Why the first time?" She asks.

"My first solo flight," I laugh, "I was so nervous I shit in my pants."

"Solo flight, meaning flying a plane?"

I nod "Yeah. A little Cessna."

"You know how to fly a plane!"

"And crap in one too."

She laughs "Like, literally, crapped? Or a wet fart?"

"No, full on - shat in my pants, two thousand feet up. I was holding the controls with one hand, and taking off of my shoes, socks, pants, and underwear with the other. The more I tried to clean it up, the more it got all over. The cabin smelled like a sewer. My instructor kept firing off questions over the radio about the flight, what's my altitude? What's my speed? I took a jug of water from behind the back seat, poured it on my shirt, and cleaned the cabin as best as I could while I answered his questions. I ended up tossing all my clothes out the window."

Mercedes and I are now laughing so hard, we're crying, "I landed an hour later butt naked, Mom and Dad waiting by the airfield – ready to take pictures."

"Oh, my god, does it feel good to laugh," Mercedes says, still laughing.

"That's exactly what Mom and Dad kept saying on the drive home."

60

Rusty

Sobriety is a harsh reality. My heart isn't listening to the commands I send – instead, it pounds against my chest begging for a hit of weed or a drink. *Just give me something, anything but this bullshit breathing you're trying*. It's an internal mind fuck; arguing with yourself. I tell the devil in my mind to shut the fuck up, and try to meditate with my eyes open – it doesn't work. All the crazy shit I've done, I've never been this nervous.

I've been sitting on this outside bench for over an hour staring at the large dental office across the parking lot. *Come on, you have time, run across the street and grab a cold one.* Fuck you. I focus on my breath, inhaling as deeply as I can, and then letting it out as slowly as I can. I commit to doing this twenty-five times.

On my twenty-first breath I start to feel high as I watch a pretty twenty-five year old walk out of the building. A jolt stops me mid-breath. It's her, and she's heading towards an old Honda Civic. The pounding in my chest is back. *This is a bad idea - you don't want to do this*. I get up faster than I intended to and yell, "Bunny."

She stops and turns towards me. I walk quickly. She doesn't recognize me. Is she scared? I stop ten feet away. "It's me," I say. And for a brief second, she looks happy to see me – it doesn't last. Her expression goes cold.

"What do you want?" she asks.

I walk closer, "Your brother is innocent, Bunny. He was set up. We have proof. He was right – I was wrong. Hell, we were all wrong. I needed you to know in case something happens. There are some very bad people that will come after me, if I don't play this out the right way. Your brother is innocent."

My baby girl tilts her head back and looks into the sky trying not to cry. She opens her mouth as if to say something, then closes it when a tear drop escapes her eye and runs down her cheek, carrying some of her mascara with it.

"When are you ever going to grow up?" she raises her voice. "You're a fifty-year-old man living in a club house, for Christ sake," she's looking directly into my eyes. "Maybe if you had been a dad he wouldn't have become a meth head."

I lower my voice, feeling only a tiny fraction of the pain I have caused her. "I know I sucked as a dad. I have no excuses for the past. But Bunny, I've put down the bottle, stopped the drugs, stopped the bullshit. I've stopped it all."

She laughs as more tears drop down her cheeks. "How many times have you said that before? Don't be an asshole."

"It's different. I'm going to meetings this time, I'm asking for help."

"Oh great. So you're here for money," she says, opening her purse.

I place my hand on top of her arm that's frantically going through the purse. She freezes. "No Bunny. I'm not here for your money. I'm here to tell you about your brother. And that I love you," I say as a tear falls from my eye. "I'm probably going to be living off grid for a while, till we get this straightened out. I had to see you first." I hand her an envelope with the little cash I have left. "Its for my grandchild," I say, taking a step forward and opening my arms. Bunny opens her arms and we hug for the first time in twenty years. I hold her tight, tears rolling off my eyes. "Thank you, Bunny.

61

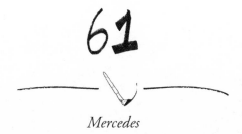

Mercedes

I'm alone. I'm cornered. They're coming towards me. "Noooooo", I scream. I look up to see if I can grab hold of something, anything to climb out of this room. "Who are you? What do you want?" There are three of them and the middle one responds to my questions by reaching into his jacket pocket and pulling out a gun. "Nathan," I yell as loudly as I can. "Nathan. The men in the black suits are here." One of them grabs hold of my arms from the back. There must be a fourth. "Leave me alone."

"Mercedes. It's me, wake up. You're having a bad dream."

I open my eyes and see Nathan standing over me. I'm in the passenger seat of the Jetta, my seat is all the way down and a sweatshirt covers me like a blanket. I hear waves.

"You okay?"

"Yeah," I say getting out of the Jetta. "Can I get a hug?" Nathan wraps his arms around me. "Thanks," I say looking out at the water. "Where are we?"

"Baker Beach. Check that out," Nathan says pointing towards a huge bridge. "Golden Gate Bridge."

"Oh my God. This is beautiful." I walk away from Nathan, looking at the bridge towering over the beach. The sun is starting to go down. "Do I have time to paint?"

"You want to paint or sketch?"

"With these colors – paint." I look at him. "But, if you're in a rush, I guess I could just do a quick sketch."

Nathan looks up and down the beach. "I'll go for a run, then grab some food for dinner," he kisses me goodbye and takes off.

I set up my easel and go to work trying to capture God's colors on my canvas, mixing blues, greens, yellows and reds. The more I mix, the better I feel. Sketching is a fun quick fix for me, but painting is my happy place. Nothing compares to the experience of mixing the colors and having them come alive on a bare canvas.

"You did it," Nathan's expression agrees with his words and it gives me goose bumps. He's holding a large white bag. "Thai food," he says and kisses me. "I'll set it up on the picnic table."

62

Nathan

After dinner we check into a Marriott in the oldest part of San Francisco. I had Mercedes wait at a coffee shop so the front desk wouldn't tie the two of us together. This city doesn't seem like a paparazzi kind of place, but I don't want to take any chances. I have to use my driver's license to check in and I'm banking on the fact that with my new haircut the front desk won't put together the fact that I am half of the Dynamic Duo. I have the same name as the kid in the news, I'll tell her if she asks. She doesn't.

We walk around the city checking out all the Art Galleries we can find. Mercedes is shocked to see a painting of the Golden Gate Bridge for sale for two thousand five hundred dollars. I am not. "We could sell them yours tomorrow morning," I say.

"Wow. Can you imagine?" she says as we walk out of the gallery.

Now we're back in the room waiting for room service to bring us two hot fudge sundaes.

"You want to watch a movie?" Mercedes asks.

"We've never done that, have we?"

"First time for everything," she smiles, sitting on the couch in her cut-off purple sweats and white tank top that she calls her sleep wear – she's beyond sexy.

I find the remote and turn on the TV to see what movies are available to rent. The CNN logo is on the bottom right of the screen. My photo fills the rest of the screen.

"Nathan Paddington might not be the saint America thinks he is," the screen cuts to a photo of Mercedes, "and Mercedes Roberts may be the mastermind behind the murders of Jack and Julie Paddington. Our reporters have discovered that the California police are working with the FBI and may be getting ready to issue a warrant for the arrest of The Dynamic Duo."

Knock. Knock. Knock.

I point to the bathroom, Mercedes runs into it and I look through the peephole, a server is holding a round tray with our two hot-fudge sundaes on it. "One sec," I say, and pull two twenties from my front pocket.

I open the door. "Here you go," I say, putting the two twenties on the tray and taking the sundaes off. "Keep the change," I say as I shut the door.

Knock. Knock. Knock. "What about the spoons?" the server asks behind the closed door.

I open the door one more time. "Thanks," I say grabbing them. "Watching a really good movie and don't want to miss anything." Hoping he gets the hint to take off.

"You can pause the movies. You want me to show you?" He takes a step forward.

"No, thank you," I shut the door, feeling it hit his feet and walk to the bathroom.

"Come on. We've got to get out of here. Quick," I say, stuffing my loose clothing into my backpack and closing it up. "Let's go. Let's go." Mercedes runs out of the bathroom with her stuff and tosses it into her pack.

"Ready," she says.

"Try to look relaxed," I say.

We walk out of the room and head down the hallway as fast as we can without jogging to the elevator and push the down button. An agonizing wait – ding. Finally the elevator completes the journey to the fifteenth floor to pick us up. We step in and I push the button for the lobby.

"Don't we want the garage?" Mercedes asks, standing shoulder-to-shoulder next to me.

"The valet puts the plate numbers, room numbers and names on each ticket. It will take the police less then five minutes to track us to this hotel and another minute for the Jetta connection."

The elevator stops – tenth floor. We can hear them first. Ding. Laughing and chanting: chug, chug, chug. The doors open – six guys in their late twenties, all wearing suits and all very drunk look in at us.

"Well, hallelujah," the closest one yells, looking straight at

Mercedes – his eyes wide open.

Mercedes steps back until her back hits the elevator wall. *My god, look at her. She's dressed for bed, for our movie night. She had just taken a shower and put on something comfy. We were in such a rush to leave the room I hadn't noticed.* The shoulder straps from her backpack are pulling her white tank top even tighter around her chest, making a perfect mold of each breast and, with no bra on, it leaves little to the imagination.

They all pile in and somehow I allow myself to get pushed to the side.

"You mind if we face this way," a guy says staring at Mercedes' chest and holding a plastic cup that he keeps spilling.

"Dressed like that, she wants us looking," another one says, stepping closer to her. "You probably want some touching too. Don't you?" he continues.

I see the fear build in Mercedes' eyes. My blood is boiling.

"How much for all of us?" another asks, reaching for her chest.

I see another hand move towards the door. The elevator thumps to a stop. No ding.

I drop my pack to the floor knowing I have no chance of taking them all on in such close quarters, but I'll do everything in my power to maim them.

"Get your fucking hand away from me!" Mercedes yells in a deafening voice that stops both me and them dead in our tracks. Her green eyes, which have always sparkled, now radiate hatred towards the men. She shows no fear.

"You want to fuck with me!" She says, standing tall and taking a step forward, her eyes narrow, her voice full of authority and confidence.

The guy that had reached for her breast takes a step back.

"Shane, Bill, knock it the fuck off. It's my wedding and you're not going to fuck this up too," the tallest one yells as he grabs the collar of the guy closest to Mercedes with one hand and pushes the emergency button with the other hand. We start moving back down again.

"Just having a little fun," the guy that was pulled away says.

Mercedes glares at the only other guy who is still facing her.

"Turn around asshole," her voice even lower and more powerful then before.

"Maybe you shouldn't dress like that," he says, turning back to his buddies as the elevator dings letting us know we've reached the lobby and the doors open. The guys pile out as if nothing had happened. "To the bar, gentlemen – to the bar," the guy getting married says.

I pick my pack up and put it on. Mercedes still hasn't looked at me. She walks out of the elevator and heads for the front entrance. I follow her. We walk two blocks until I can't take it anymore.

"Mercedes," I say. "Stop. Talk to me. You okay?"

"It shouldn't matter what I have on. If I want to look sexy for you or for me, so be it. That doesn't give anyone the right to violate me," her voice starts cracking, her eyes well up.

"Hey," I say pulling her into a hug.

"I was so scared, Nathan."

"You were amazing."

"I knew you were going to go after them. I was scared of losing you. Of losing us," she says, kissing me. I open my mouth, kissing her back. We get lost in each other.

"We'd better get going," I pull away from her.

"I… eh," she looks down at her tank top that is now damp from sweat and would win first prize in a spring break wet T-shirt contest. "We don't need any more attention."

I laugh, forgetting for a second that we may in fact be on the run.

"There's a Gap right up there," I say pointing to the next corner. "It looks like it might still be open."

63

"Welcome to the Gap, we close in ten minutes," the girl behind the counter says, mechanically looking up and then back down to continue whatever it is she is doing.

A scrawny Hispanic kid in skinny jeans walks up to us. "Well, hello handsome couple, what can I get for you?" He looks at Mercedes' shirt and smiles. "You go girl. Could I please come back as sexy as you."

Mercedes smiles. "I need a shirt and a pair of jeans," she says walking up to the table of sweatshirts.

"Don't you be covering up." He turns to me. "Why don't we dress him down to match," he laughs. "My name's Victor. Friends call me Vickie," he extends his hand.

"I'm going to try these on, Vickie," Mercedes leaves us for the dressing room.

"You live in town, Vickie?"

He laughs. "Can't live in this town with retail wages. Nope, I live east of Oakland."

"Don't they have Gaps in Oakland?"

"Baby, I don't come to San Francisco for the Gap – I come for the night life."

"What you got going on tonight?" I ask.

Vickie's eyes light up as he checks me out real slow top to bottom. "Well, until the after-hours party, I could rearrange my commitments. What do you have in mind?"

"We need a ride," I say.

His expression instantly changes. "A ride. Damn, boy. You got me all worked up."

"Well, what do you think," Mercedes says walking out of the dressing room.

"Plain Jane," Vickie says. "How dare you waste those looks on these clothes!" he says just above a whisper.

"Hi Jane," I say to her. Then to Vickie, "What time does your after-hours party start?"

"One-thirty," he says, turning away from Mercedes with an odd expression.

"I'll give you three hundred dollars cash if you drive us to Discovery Bay. If we leave in the next twenty minutes you should get back an hour before your party."

"I'll be ready in ten", he says.

64

Vickie has an old red Lincoln Continental, with white leather seats and custom white shag carpet. It's in mint condition and fully decked out with the best stereo system I've ever heard in a car. He's playing what he calls thumper music, a combination of electronic dance and old-time rock and roll without the lyrics.

"Retail seems to be treating you right," I say.

"That's just my respectable front, you know, keep the government off my back – pay my fair share of taxes, right?" he laughs.

"So is driving us out here a pay cut?" I ask.

"Darling, I get three hundred an hour and I'm busy. A lot of rich straight boys come to San Fran for a little play. I'm their tour guide."

"So why are you doing this for us?" Mercedes asks.

"Baby, you may be one bright girl, but you are no mastermind for murder." He turns to me and says "And you sure are not capable of such a heinous crime. I grew up in the projects. I know what killers look like and you ain't no killer."

So what's his plan for us? I wondered.

"It's those *National Geographic* green eyes of yours," he says, looking into the rear-view mirror at Mercedes. And then, turning to me, "and those high cheek bones of yours. Individually, I wouldn't have figured it out, but the two of you together. Yeah. I knew I'd seen you before, but couldn't pinpoint it. Then, when you came out of the dressing room in those plain Jane clothes, all I could see were your eyes – and it hit me." He turns to me. "That shot of her online, leaning against the Harley – her eyes looking straight into the camera lens. You had that same look when you came out of the dressing room looking at Nathan."

"So much for our disguises," I say.

"You're safe with me.

We pass a sign that reads "Welcome to Discovery Bay". I see Mercedes going through her pack. "How about that coffee shop up on the left?" I suggest.

65

Vickie won't take any money for the ride. Instead, he gives us his cell number, home address and his word he won't tell anyone about us. I believe him; but still, I don't want him or anyone else knowing we are headed to Stockton.

Mercedes puts her brown contacts back in, and walks into the coffee shop. I go to the CVS across the street and buy a disposable phone and call Rusty's home number. It goes to a recording, "Out and about. Leave it at the tone."

"Hi Rusty, it's me."

He picks up. "Where you at?"

I give him the address.

"Be there in half an hour."

Mercedes and I share a sandwich and salad. Without her green eyes, I'm no longer worried about being spotted. I realize now we shouldn't have run from the hotel. We have nothing to hide except the thumb drive. Now we look guilty.

I look across the table at Mercedes. She smiles. My heart skips a beat. I love her even more then I loved my parents. Mom always told me that would happen, that one day, if I were open and honest with myself, I'd find the person that would complete me. She said an honest intimate relationship was the greatest gift life had to offer.

"What?" Mercedes says, smiling at me. "You have this funny look. What are you thinking about?"

"I'll be right back," I grab my pack and head to the bathroom, leaving Mercedes with a confused look on her face.

A minute later I'm back sitting in front of Mercedes again.

"What?" she asks.

"Tomorrow morning I'm going to call Dad's lawyer, Paul White, and get this mess straightened out. We shouldn't have run from the hotel. I wasn't thinking clearly. This whole dynamic duo crap, the thumb drive, your biological dad being a dick, the bombing in Saratoga Springs, it all snowballed, and when I saw the news it freaked me out. We don't need to run from anything, Mercedes. We have each other and our entire lives ahead of us. I don't care what's on the thumb drive - Rusty can do whatever he wants with it. We've both been through enough. I'm done running."

Mercedes leans her head back and with the tips of her fingers she takes the brown contacts off of her eyes. "I like that idea. " Her green eyes coming alive again.

I get up from my chair, "Mercedes," I say dropping to one knee. "Would you make me the happiest person on the face of the planet by being my wife so we can share our lives, explore the world, do some good, and start a family together?" I'm so nervous I almost drop the ring I bought at the hotel gift shop.

"Yes. Yes!" Mercedes says and drops down to her knees, tears in her eyes. "Yes, I would love to share my life with you, more than anything in this world."

We kiss. A few customers on the far side of the shop clap. We sit back down at the table holding hands. We're both glowing.

Twenty minutes later we see Rusty's car pull in front of the coffee shop, but he's not driving … or is he? Mercedes and I look closer at the driver's seat and giggle. "Looks like you're not the only clean-cut guy," Mercedes elbows me.

I ask her to go outside first to see if he recognizes her. He doesn't.

I grab both our packs and walk outside as Rusty gets out of the car. "Nice haircut," I say.

He doesn't do a double take, but looks surprised at my new look. "Didn't think you could look any younger, "he says. "You do."

I open the back door and toss the packs in the back. I'm excited and can't wait to share the news.

"What the fuck you so happy about?" Rusty asks.

"We just need to wait for Mercedes," I say getting into the car and looking at Mercedes leaning against the coffee shop wall with her baseball cap, black glasses and new ring on her finger.

"Where the hell is she?" He asks, getting into the driver's seat.

"Don't know, but that's a cute girl, isn't she?" I say pointing to Mercedes and laughing.

"No shit. For real?"

"Yep," I open the car door, "come on."

Mercedes hops in and we take off laughing.

"We have a lot to cover and not a lot of time," Rusty says as he accelerates onto the highway. "You guys are all over the news and none of it's any good."

Mercedes leans forward, "Rusty, we have some good news. Some really good news. Nathan and I are getting married."

"You're what?" He looks at me.

"We're doing it," I say.

Rusty looks back at the road. I can't tell if he's happy for us or not.

"I'm going to call my dad's lawyer first thing tomorrow and get this whole arrest thing straightened out." I look at Rusty. "This whole media thing, the Dynamic Duo thing, has taught us that we don't want to be on the run. We don't want to be known. We just want to be. The thumb drive is yours to do whatever you want with. You can toss it, sell it or give it away. We can't handle any more drama."

Rusty's grip on the steering wheel seems to tighten. Yes, it is getting tighter. He's not happy.

"We thought you'd be happy for us," I say, trying to snap him out of it and wondering why I even called him to pick us up.

"You know my son Jimmy is in prison for life, right?"

Not sure I like where this is going. "Yes, you told me," I answer.

Still holding the wheel firmly and staring straight ahead, Rusty says, "He swore up and down he'd been set up. No one believed him, including myself. Your thumb drive has information that can get him out of prison. That's why I sent it out from rehab, I couldn't sit on it." He looks at Mercedes. "I knew how excited you were to meet your dad and I didn't want to put a dark cloud on that experience."

"Yeah, Dad turned out to be a real champ," Mercedes says. "He's more like a tsunami than a dark cloud."

Rusty takes a moment. His grip softens on the wheel. "Sorry to hear that," his voice full of emotion.

"But why did you send it from the rehab? You knew they'd be able to track it back."

"My roommate was a real dickhead. He was constantly bragging about being with underage girls, so I sent the photos from his computer knowing that, if the information was as dangerous as your dad said it was, he could be taken out." He glances at me. "I hope to have a granddaughter soon. I didn't have a problem if they tracked down a child molester and took him out. But I had no idea they'd take out the entire rehab facility – two full blocks. This is some seriously deep shit."

"Who did you send it to?" I ask.

"CNN, *Fox*, the *New York Times*, and every other major news outlet."

"Did they all pick it up?" I ask.

"None of them did," he lets one hand drop from the wheel to his lap.

"Wow. None of them?" Mercedes asks.

"Zilch. But, I also sent it to a bunch of blogs," Rusty smiles.

"And?" I ask.

"And," he pauses for dramatic effect, "pay day. It's creating a firestorm. The mainstream media are going to have to pick it up or at least call it out as fake news."

We pull into Rusty's garage, "I am happy for you two," he turns to me. "Really happy."

"Do you know any priests or justices of the peace that will marry us tomorrow?" I ask, glowing with excitement.

"Matter a fact I do. Guy at the club house is a licensed Justice of the Peace."

66

Just before Rusty turns the knob to go inside, he looks back at Mercedes and me and says, "don't be freaked out," and then pushes the door open.

The inside looks like a scene out of a C.S.I. episode. Photos of politicians, police officers, CEOs and professional athletes line his living room walls. The Governor of California is at the top, the President of the United States is below him, the Secretary of State is the third photo.

"Wow, you've been busy," I say.

"Where's the bathroom?" Mercedes asks.

"Down the hall to the right," Rusty says. "I'll get us some drinks." He heads to the kitchen. Mercedes heads to the bathroom.

I walk over and look at the photos on the wall. Rusty comes

back with three Snapple Ice Teas and hands me one. "Thanks," I say opening the bottle. "What's the information on the President?" I ask.

"A lot, and its not just about him. The guy is married and has two ex wives. He was a civilian his entire life until he became president. His kids are all in their thirties. They grew up rich, they traveled, and they did some crazy shit. The President too. Six hundred pages documenting the crazy shit they all did, with photos that will destroy them politically if they get out."

Mercedes comes back in. Rusty hands her a Snapple. "Thanks," she says looking at the wall, "Wow."

"You obviously have a plan. What is it?" I ask.

"Take down the Governor first so I can get Jimmy out of jail."

I nod my head.

"He's hosting a gala in two weeks, I'm going to make contact with him then and make him an offer he can't refuse," he says staring at the Governor's photo.

67

It's just after midnight. Mercedes and I are pulling out the couch to make up the bed. We have smiles pasted on our faces. Rusty called his friend who's a Justice of the Peace and set us up for 3 o'clock tomorrow.

"I'm so excited," I say, tucking the corner of the sheet under the mattress.

"Me too," she says, green eyes sparkling. "What?" She asks.

"It's weird. Cause with everything we've been through, I've never been so happy in my life."

She comes closer, her purple shorts back on, a clean white tank top. Her beauty sends tingles throughout my body. I step even closer looking deep into her eyes. She bends her arms up, elbows to her sides, with her palms out facing me. I do the same. She takes one more step. Our palms join together. Our chests start to rise and fall together. I feel her breasts brush up against my chest as our breathing becomes one. I kiss her on the lips as softly as I can. She kisses me back. Our hips join together. I feel a tear on my cheek. It's not mine.

"Hey," I say, lifting her chin up with my hand. "What's with the tears?"

"I'm just so happy I saved myself for this moment, for you, for tomorrow night."

The energy that shoots through me is like nothing I'd ever experienced. I kiss her forehead.

She whispers "Tomorrow night," in my ear and climbs into bed.

I go to the bathroom and take an extra blanket out of the closet and stretch it out on the floor and get under it. I use my sweatshirt for a pillow. I still can't get this smile off my face.

"I already miss you," she says.

"This will be fun to tell our kids," I say.

"I love you," She says.

"I love you," I say.

68

I wake up – a smile still glued to my face. It's 5:30 am. I do my push-ups, squats, and sit-ups. Mercedes is still asleep, so I start my meditation.

I open my eyes, it's 6:00 am, Mercedes is sitting up in bed – her smile still pasted on her face too. I walk over and kiss her on the forehead; then I tell her, "I'm going to go online real quick and check out one of my dad's lessons and then call Paul White."

"Okay," she giggles, "I'm so excited."

"Me too."

I go over to Rusty's computer and move the mouse to wake it up. With the screen alive I type in the Secure URL my dad made me memorize and wait for the page to come up. I miss him and Mom so much. The home page pops up. I type in my user name and password and hit the return button. Rusty must have a slow connection cause it seems to be taking longer. A photo of my dad pops up on screen with a triangle "Play" button on it. "What the hell?" All the other URL's that were on the page before are gone. *Someone has hacked into this.* I think I hear Mercedes say something, but am not sure because the photo of my dad has a newspaper in it with yesterday's date on it. I move the cursor over the "Play" button. *Who would do this? Who could do this?* I click the mouse starting the video.

"Nathan! Stop sending out the photos, you're going to get us killed - We're alive, Nathan."

About the Author

Warren Shumway has commercial fished in Alaska, was a professional tree climber, acted in New York City and founded an adventure employment agency in Los Angeles called ActionJobs that he sold in 2004. He enjoys skiing, motorcycles, white water kayaking and hiking. He has traveled to Southeast East Asia, Poland, Pakistan, India and south America. This is Warren's first novel. If you'd like to be contacted on his next book, send an email to warrenshumway@gmail.com

43300557R00146

Made in the USA
Lexington, KY
27 June 2019